The three travelers studied the map of
the Black Zone. Reith, the Earthman,
touched down his finger. "Here we are,"
he said. "The Dirdir must pass yonder,
west of the woods, which is our destination."

"No doubt our destiny as well," remarked Anacho, the Dirdirman renegade,
with a pessimistic sniff.

"I would as soon die killing Dirdir as
any other way," said Traz.

"One does not die killing Dirdir," Anacho corrected delicately. "They do not permit it."

The Dirdir

JACK VANCE

DAW BOOKS, INC.

DONALD A. WOLLHEIM, PUBLISHER

New York

FIRST DAW PRINTING, JULY 1979

1 2 3 4 5 6 7 8 9

 DAW TRADEMARK REGISTERED
U.S. PAT. OFF. MARCA
REGISTRADA. HECHO EN U.S.A.

PRINTED IN U.S.A.

PRELIMINARY

Two HUNDRED and twelve light-years from Earth hung the smoky yellow star Carina 4269 and its single planet Tschai. Coming to investigate a mysterious surge of radio signals, the survey ship *Explorator IV* met destruction. The sole survivor, star-scout Adam Reith, was rescued, barely alive, by Traz Onmale, boy-chief of the Emblem nomads.

From the first, Adam Reith's urgent goal was to return to Earth, with news of Tschai and its queer conglomeration of peoples. In his quest for a suitable spaceship he was joined by Traz, then by one Ankhe at afram Anacho, a fugitive Dirdirman.

Tschai, so Reith learned, had been the scene of ancient wars between three off-world races: the Dirdir, the Chasch, and the Wankh. An uneasy stalemate now existed, each race maintaining an area of influence, with the vast hinterlands abandoned to nomads, fugitives, bandits, feudal lords, and a few more or less civilized communities. Indigenous to Tschai were the solitary Phung and the Pnume, a furtive race occupying caverns, tunnels, and passages under the ruined cities which marked the Tschai landscape.

Each of the alien races had indentured or enslaved men who across thousands of years had evolved toward the host race, so that now there were Dirdirmen, Chaschmen, Wankhmen and Pnumekin, in addition to other, more obviously human, peoples.

From the first Reith had marveled at the presence of men on Tschai. One evening at a Dead Steppe caravansary the Dirdirman Anacho clarified the matter: "Before the Chasch came, the Pnume ruled everywhere. They lived in villages of little domes, but all traces of these are gone. Now they keep to caves and dark fastnesses, and their lives are a mystery. Even the Dirdir consider it bad luck to molest a Pnume."

"The Chasch came to Tschai before the Dirdir?" Reith asked.

"This is well-known," said Anacho, wondering at Reith's ignorance. "The first invaders were Old Chasch, a hundred thousand years ago. Ten thousand years later the Blue Chasch arrived, from a planet colonized an era earlier by previous Chasch spacefarers. The two Chasch races fought for Tschai, and brought in Green Chasch for shock troops.

"Sixty thousand years ago the Dirdir appeared in force. The Chasch suffered great losses until the Dirdir arrived in large numbers and themselves became vulnerable, whereupon a stalemate went into effect. The races are still enemies with little traffic between them.

"Comparatively recently, ten thousand years ago, space-war broke out between the Dirdir and the Wankh, and extended to Tschai when the Wankh built forts on Rakh and South Kachan. Now there is little fighting, other than skirmishes and ambushes. Each race fears the other and bides its time. The Pnume are neutral and take no part in the wars, though they watch all with interest and make memoirs for their great history."

"What of man?" Reith asked guardedly. "When did they arrive on Tschai?"

"Men originated," said the Dirdirman in his most didactic manner, "on Sibol and came to Tschai with the Dirdir. Men are as plastic as wax. Some metamorphosed, first into marshmen, then, twenty thousand years ago, into his sort." Here Anacho indicated Traz, who glowered back. "Others, enslaved, became Chaschmen, Pnumekin, even Wankhmen. There are dozens of hybrids and freakish races. Variety exists even among the Dirdirmen. The Immaculates, for instance, are almost pure Dirdir. Others exhibit less refinement. This is the background for my own disaffection: I demanded prerogatives which were denied me but which I adopted in any event . . ."

Anacho spoke on, describing his difficulties, but Reith's attention wandered. It was now clear how men had come to Tschai. The Dirdir had known space-travel for more than seventy thousand years. During this time they had evidently visited Earth, twice at the very least. On the first occasion they had captured a tribe of proto-Mongoloids—the apparent nature of the marshmen to which Anacho had alluded. On the second occasion—twenty thousand years ago, according to Anacho—they had collected a cargo of proto-Caucasoids. These two groups, under the special conditions of Tschai, had mutated, specialized, re-mutated, respecialized, to produce the bewildering complexity of human types now to be found on the planet.

Unsuccessful in an attempt to commandeer a Wankh spaceship, Reith and his companions take refuge at Smargash, in the Lokhar Highlands of Kachan.

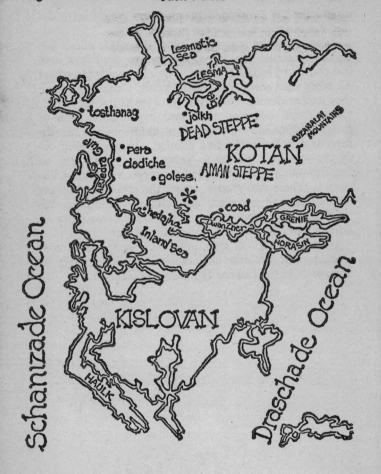

CHARCHAN

CATH
• settra
• ballisidre

KACHAN RAKH

VORD

TSCHAI
✳ WHERE SPACE BOAT CRASHED

Chapter 1

The sun Carina 4269 had passed into the constellation Tartusz, to mark the onset of Balul Zac Ag, the "unnatural dream time," when slaughter, slave-taking, pillage and arson came to a halt across the Lokhar Highlands. Balul Zac Ag was the occasion for the Great Fair at Smargash, or perhaps the Great Fair had come first, eventually to generate Balul Zac Ag after unknown hundreds of years. From across the Lokhar Highlands and the regions surrounding Xar, Zhurveg, Serafs, Niss and others came to Smargash to mingle and trade, to resolve stale feuds, to gather intelligence. Hatred hung in the air like a stench; covert glances and whispered curses, in-drawn hisses of detestation accented the color and confusion of the bazaar. Only the Lokhars (the men black-skinned and white-haired, the women white-skinned and black-haired) maintained faces of placid unconcern.

On the second day of Balul Zac Ag, as Adam Reith wandered through the bazaar, he became aware that he was being watched. The knowledge came as a dismal shock; on Tschai, surveillance always led to a grim conclusion.

Perhaps he was mistaken, Reith told himself. He had dozens of enemies; to many others he represented ideological disaster; but how could any of these have traced him to Smargash? Reith continued along the crowded lanes of the bazaar, pausing at the booths to look back the way he had come. But his follower, if in fact he existed, was lost in the confusion. There were Niss in black robes, seven feet tall, striding like rapacious birds; Xars; Serafs; Dugbo nomads squatting over their fires; Human Things expressionless behind

11

pottery face-plates; Zhurvegs in coffee-brown kaftans;
the black and white Lokhars of Smargash themselves.
There was odd staccato noise: the clank of iron,
squeak of leather, harsh voices, shrill calls, the whine,
rasp and jangle of Dugbo music. There were odors:
fern-spice, gland-oil, sub-musk, dust rising and settling,
the reek of prickled nuts, smoke from grilled meats, the
perfume of the Serafs. There were colors: black, dull
brown, orange, old scarlet, dark blue, dark gold. Leaving the bazaar Reith crossed the dancing field. He
stopped short, and from the corner of his eye glimpsed
a figure sliding behind a tent.

Thoughtfully Reith returned to the inn. Traz and the
Dirdirman, Ankhe at afram Anacho, sat in the refectory making a meal of bread and meat. They ate in
silence; disparate beings, each found the other incom-
prehensible. Anacho, tall, thin and pallid like all
Dirdirmen, was completely hairless, a quality he now
tended to minimize under a soft tasseled cap after the
style of the Yao. His personality was unpredictable; he
inclined toward garrulity, freakish jokes, sudden petu-
lances. Traz, square, somber and sturdy, was in most
respects Anacho's obverse. Traz considered Anacho
vain, over-subtle, over-civilized; Anacho thought Traz
tactless, severe and over-literal. How the two managed
to travel in comparative amity was a mystery to Reith.

Reith seated himself at the table. "I think I'm being
watched," he announced.

Anacho leaned back in dismay. "Then we must
prepare for disaster—or flight."

"I prefer flight," said Reith. He poured himself ale
from a stone jug.

"You still intend to travel space to this mythical
planet of yours?" Anacho spoke in the voice of one
who reasons with an obstinate child.

"I want to return to Earth, certainly."

"Bah," muttered Anacho. "You are the victim of a
hoax, or an obsession. Can you not cure yourself? The
project is easier to discuss than to effectuate.

Spaceships are not wart-scissors, to be picked up at any bazaar booth."

Reith said sadly, "I know this only too well."

Anacho spoke in an offhand manner: "I suggest that you apply at the Grand Sivishe Spaceyards. Almost anything can be procured, if one has enough sequins."

"I suspect that I don't," said Reith.

"Go to the Carabas. Sequins can be had by the bucketful."

Traz gave a short snort of derision. "Do you take us for maniacs?"

"Where is the Carabas?" asked Reith.

"The Carabas is in the Dirdir Hunting Preserve, at the north of Kislovan. Men with luck and strong nerves sometimes prosper."

"Fools, gamblers and murderers, rather," muttered Traz.

Reith asked, "How do these men, whatever their nature, gain the sequins?"

Anacho's voice was flippant and airy. "By the usual method: they dig up nodes of chrysospine."

Reith rubbed his chin. "Is this the source of sequins? I thought that the Dirdir or some such folk minted them."

"Your ignorance is that of another planet indeed!" declared Anacho.

The muscles around Reith's mouth gave a rueful twitch. "It could hardly be otherwise."

"The chrysospine," said Anacho, "grows only in the Black Zone, which is to say, the Carabas, where uranium compounds occur in the soil. A full node yields two hundred and eighty-two sequins, of one or another color. A purple sequin is worth a hundred clears; a scarlet is fifty, and down through the emeralds, blues, sards and milks. Even Traz knows as much."

Traz looked at Anacho with a curled lip. " 'Even Traz'?"

Anacho paid him no heed. "All this to the side; we

have no certain evidence of surveillance. Adam Reith may well be mistaken."

"Adam Reith is not mistaken," said Traz. " 'Even Traz,' as you put it, knows better than this."

Anacho raised his hairless eyebrows. "How so?"

"Notice the man who just entered the room."

"A Lokhar; what about him?"

"He is no Lokhar. He watches our every move."

Anacho's jaw fell a trifle slack.

Reith studied the man surreptitiously; he seemed less burly, less direct and abrupt than the typical Lokhar. Anacho spoke in a subdued voice: "The lad is right. Notice how he drinks his ale, head down instead of back. . . . Disturbing."

Reith muttered, "Who would be interested in us?"

Anacho gave a bark of caustic laughter. "Do you think that our exploits have gone unnoticed? The events at Ao Hidis have aroused attention everywhere."

"So this man—whom would he serve?"

Anacho shrugged. "With his skin dyed black I can't even guess his breed."

"We'd better get some information," said Reith. He considered a moment. "I'll walk out through the bazarr, then around into the Old Town. If the man yonder follows, give him a start and come behind. If he stays, one of you stay, the other come after me."

Reith went out into the bazaar. At a Zhurveg pavilion he paused to examine a display of rugs, woven, according to rumor, by legless children, kidnapped and maimed by the Zhurvegs themselves. He glanced back the way he had come. No one appeared to be following. He went on a little way, and paused by the racks where hideous Niss women sold coils of braided leather rope, leap-horse harness, crudely beautiful silver goblets. Still no one behind. He crossed the passage to examine a Dugbo display of musical instruments. If he could take a cargo of Zhurveg rugs, Niss silver, Dugbo musical instruments back to Earth, thought Reith, his fortune would be made. He looked over his shoulder, and now he observed Anacho dawdling fifty yards behind. Anacho clearly had learned nothing.

Reith sauntered on. He paused to watch a Dugbo necromancer: a twisted old man squatting behind trays of misshapen bottles, jugs of salve, junction-stones to facilitate telepathy, love-sticks, sheafs of curses indited on red and green paper. Above flew a dozen fantastic kites, which the old Dugbo manipulated to produce a wan wailing music. He proffered Reith an amulet, which Reith refused to buy. The necromancer spat epithets and caused his kites to dart and shriek discords.

Reith moved on, into the Dugbo encampment proper. Girls wearing scarves and flounced skirts of black, old rose and ocher solicited Zhurvegs, Lokhars, Serafs, but taunted the prudish Niss who stalked silently past, heads out-thrust, noses like scythes of polished bone. Beyond the encampment lay the open plain and the far hills, black and gold in the light of Carina 4269.

A Dugbo girl approached Reith, jangling the silver ornaments at her waist, smiling a gap-toothed grin. "What do you seek out here, my friend? Are you weary? This is my tent; enter, refresh yourself."

Reith declined the invitation and stepped back before her fingers or those of her younger sisters could flutter near his pouch.

"Why are you reluctant?" sang the girl. "Look at me! Am I not graceful? I have polished my limbs with Seraf wax; I am scented with haze-water; you could do far worse!"

"No doubt whatever," said Reith. "Still . . ."

"We will talk together, Adam Reith! We will tell each other of many strange matters."

"How do you know my name?" demanded Reith.

The girl waved her scarf at the younger girls, as if at insects. "Who at Smargash does not know Adam Reith, who strides abroad like an Ilanth prince, and his mind always full of thoughts?"

"I am notorious, then?"

"Oh, indeed. Must you go?"

"Yes, I have an engagement." Reith continued on his way. The girl watched after him with an odd half-smile, which Reith, looking over his shoulder, found disconcerting.

A few hundred yards further along, Anacho approached from a side-lane. "The man dyed like a Lokhar remained at the inn. For a period you were followed by a young woman dressed as a Dugbo. In the encampment she accosted you, then followed no more."

"Strange," muttered Reith. He looked up and down the street. "No one follows us now?"

"No one is visible. We might well be under observation. Turn about, if you will."

Anacho ran his long white fingers over the fabric of Reith's jacket. "So I suspected." He displayed a small black button. "And now we know who tracks you. Do you recognize this?"

"No. But I can guess. A tell-tale."

"A Dirdir adjunct for hunting, used by the very young or the very old to guide them after their quarry."

"So the Dirdir are interested in me."

Anacho's face became long and pinched, as if he tasted something acrid. "The events at Ao Khaha have naturally attracted their attention."

"What should they want with me?"

"Dirdir motives are seldom subtle. They want to ask a few questions and then kill you."

"The time has come to move on."

Anacho glanced toward the sky. "That time has come and gone. I suspect that a Dirdir sky-car approaches at this very moment. . . . Give me the button."

A Niss approached, black robes flapping to the stride of his legs. Anacho stepped forth, made a swift movement toward the black gown. The Niss sprang around with a grunt of menace, and for a moment seemed ready to abandon the unnatural restraints of

Balul Zac Ag. Then he wheeled and continued along his way.

Anacho gave his thin fluting chuckle. "The Dirdir will be puzzled when Adam Reith proves to be a Niss."

"Before they learn differently, we had best be gone."

"Agreed, but how?"

"I suggest that we consult old Zarfo Detwiler."

"Luckily we know where to find him."

Skirting the bazaar, the two approached the ale-house, a ramshackle structure of stone and weather-beaten planks. Today Zarfo sat within, to escape the dust and confusion of the bazaar. A stone crock of ale almost hid his black-dyed face. He was dressed in unaccustomed elegance: polished black boots, a maroon cape, a black tricorn hat pulled down over his flowing white hair. He was somewhat drunk and even more garrulous than usual. With difficulty Reith made him aware of his problem. Zarfo at last became exercised. "So, the Dirdir now! Infamous, and during Balul Zac Ag! They had better control their arrogance, or know the wrath of the Lokhars!"

"All this to the side," said Reith, "how can we most quickly leave Smargash?"

Zarfo blinked and dipped another ladle of ale from the crock. "First I must learn where you wish to go."

"The Isles of Cloud, or perhaps the Carabas."

Zarfo let the ladle sag in shock. "The Lokhars are the most avaricious of people, yet how many attempt the Carabas? Few! And how many return with wealth? Have you noticed the great manor house to the east, with the chain of carved ivory around the bower?"

"I have seen the manor."

"There are no other such manors near Smargash," said Zarfo portentously. "Do you get my meaning?" He rapped on the bench. "Pot-boy! More ale."

"I mentioned the Isles of Cloud as well," said Reith.

"Tusa Tala on the Draschade is more convenient for the Isles. How to reach Tusa Tala? The motor-wagon fares only to Siadz at the edge of the highlands; I know of no route down the chasms to the Draschade. The caravan to Zara is two months gone. A sky-raft is the only sensible conveyance."

"Well, then, where can we obtain a sky-raft?"

"Not from the Lokhars; we have none. Look yonder: a sky-raft and a party of rich Xars! They are about to depart. Maybe their destination is Tusa Tala. Let us inquire."

"A moment. We must get word to Traz." Reith called the pot-boy, sent him running to the inn.

Zarfo strode out across the compound with Reith and Anacho behind. Five Xars stood by their old sky-raft: short bull-shouldered men with congested complexions. They wore rich robes of gray and green; their black hair rose in rigid varnished columns, flaring slightly outward and sheared off flat.

"Leaving Smargash so soon, friend Xars?" Zarfo called out in a cheerful voice.

The Xars muttered together and turned away.

Zarfo ignored the lack of affability. "Where then are you bound?"

"Lake Falas; where else?" declared the oldest Xar. "Our business is done; as usual we were cheated. We are anxious to return to the swamps."

"Excellent. This gentleman and his two friends need transportation to a point in your general direction. They asked me whether they should offer to pay; I said, 'Nonsense! The Xars are princes of generosity—' "

"Hold!" the Xar called sharply. "I have at least three remarks to make. First, our raft is crowded. Second, we are generous unless we lose sequins in the process. Third, these two nondescripts have a reckless and desperate air about them, not at all reassuring. Is this the third?" The reference was to Traz, who had arrived on the scene. "A mere lad but no less dubious for all that."

Another Xar spoke. "Two further questions: How much can they pay? Where do they wish to go?"

Reith, considering the uncomfortably scant supply of sequins in his pouch, said, "A hundred sequins is all we can offer; and we want to be taken to Tusa Tala."

The Xars threw up their hands in outrage. "Tusa Tala? A thousand miles northwest! We head southeast to Lake Falas! A hundred sequins? Is this a joke? Montebanks! Off with all of you!"

Zarfo swaggered threateningly forward. "A montebank, you call me? Were it not Balul Zac Ag, the 'unnatural dream time,' I would tweak all of your ludicrously long noses!"

The Xars made spitting sounds between their teeth, climbed aboard the raft and departed.

Zarfo stared after the departing raft. He heaved a sigh. "In this case, failure. . . . Well, all may not prove so churlish. In the sky comes another craft; we shall put the proposal to those aboard, or at an extremity, render them drunk and borrow the vehicle. A handsome craft, that. Surely—"

Anacho gave a startled outcry. "A Dirdir sky-car! Already they are here! Away to concealment, for our very lives!"

He started to dart away. Reith seized his arm. "Don't run; do you want them to identify us so quickly?" To Zarfo: "Where shall we hide?"

"In the ale-house storeroom—but never forget that this is Balul Zac Ag! The Dirdir would never dare violence!"

"Bah," sneered Anacho. "What do they know of your customs, or care?"

"I will explain to them," declared Zarfo. He led the three to a shed beside the ale-house, ushered them within. Through a crack in the plank Reith watched the Dirdir sky-car settle into the compound. On sudden thought he turned to Traz, felt over his garments, and in vast dismay discovered a black disk.

"Quick," said Anacho. "Give it here." He left the shed, went into the ale-house. A minute later he returned. "An old Lokhar departing for his cottage now carries the tell-tale." He went to a crack, peered out toward the field. "Dirdir, sure enough! As always when sport is to be had!"

The sky-car lay quiet: a craft different from any

Reith had seen heretofore, the product of a sure and sophisticated technology. Five Dirdir stepped to the ground: impressive creatures, harsh, mercurial, decisive. They stood approximately at human height, and moved with sinister quickness, like lizards on a hot day. Their dermal surfaces suggested polished bone; their crania raised into sharp blade-like crests, with incandescent antennae streaming back at either side. The contours of the faces were oddly human, with deep eye-sockets, the scalp crests descending to suggest nasal ridges. They half-hopped, half-loped, like leopards walking erect; it was not hard to see in them the wild creatures which had hunted the hot plains of Sibol.

Three persons approached the Dirdir: the false Lokhar, the Dugbo girl, a man in nondescript gray garments. The Dirdir spoke with the three for several minutes, then brought forth instruments, which they pointed in different directions. Anacho hissed: "They locate their tell-tales. And the old Lokhar in the ale-house still dawdles over his pot!"

"No matter," said Reith. "As well in the ale-house as anywhere else."

The Dirdir approached the ale-house, moving with their curious half-loping stride. Behind came the three spies.

The old Lokhar chose this moment to lurch from the ale-house. The Dirdir inspected him in puzzlement, and approached by great leaps. The Lokhar drew back in alarm. "What have we here? Dirdir? Don't interfere with me!"

The Dirdir spoke in sibilant lisping voices which suggested the absence of a larynx. "Do you know a man called Adam Reith?"

"Indeed not! Stand aside!"

Zarfo thrust himself forward. "Adam Reith, you say? What of him?"

"Where is he?"

"Why do you ask?"

The false Lokhar stepped forward, muttered to the

Dirdir. The Dirdir said, "You know Adam Reith well?"

"Not well. If you have money for him, leave it with me; he would have wanted it so."

"Where is he?"

Zarfo looked out across the sky. "You saw the sky-raft which departed as you arrived?"

"Yes."

"It might be that he and his friends were aboard."

"Who claims this to be true?"

"Not I," said Zarfo. "I offer only the suggestion."

"Nor I," said the old Lokhar who had carried the tell-tale.

"What is the direction?"

"Pah! You are the great trackers," sneered Zarfo. "Why ask us poor innocents?"

The Dirdir retreated across the compound in long strides. The sky-car darted off into the air.

Zarfo confronted the three Dirdir agents, his big face twisted into a malevolent grin. "So here you are in Smargash, violating our laws. Do you not know this is Balul Zac Ag?"

"We committed no violence," stated the false Lokhar, "but merely did our work."

"Dirty work, conducive to violence! You shall all be flogged. Where are the constables? I give these three into custody!"

The three agents were hustled away, protesting and crying and making demands.

Zarfo came to the shed. "Best that you leave at once. The Dirdir will not delay long." He pointed across the compound. "The wagon to the west is ready to depart."

"Where does it take us?"

"Out to the highland rim. Beyond lie the chasms! A grim territory. But if you remain here, you will be taken by the Dirdir. Balul Zac Ag or no."

Reith looked around the compound, at the dusty stone and timber structures of Smargash, at the black and white Lokhars, at the shabby old inn. Here had

been the single interim of peace and security he had
known on Tschai; now events were forcing him once
more into the unknown. In a hollow voice he said, "We
need fifteen minutes to collect our gear."

Anacho said in a dismal voice, "This situation does
not accord with my hopes. . . . But I must make the
best of it. Tschai is a world of anguish."

Chapter 2

Zarfo came to the inn with white Seraf robes and
spine helmets. "Wear these; conceivably you may win
an additional hour or two. Hurry—the wagon is at the
point of departure."

"One moment." Reith surveyed the compound.
"There may be other spies, watching our every move."

"Well, then, by the back lane. After all, we cannot
anticipate every contingency."

Reith made no further comments; Zarfo was becoming peevish and anxious to get them out of Smargash,
no matter in what direction.

Silently, each man thinking his own thoughts, they
went to the motor-wagon terminus. Zarfo told them:
"Say nothing to anyone; pretend to meditate: that is
the way of the Serafs. At sundown face the east and
utter a loud cry: 'Ah-oo-cha!' No one knows what it
means but that is the Seraf way. If pressed, state that
you come to buy essences. So then: aboard the wagon!
May you avoid the Dirdir and succeed in all your future undertakings. And if not, remember that death
comes only once!"

"Thank you for the consolation," said Reith.

The motor-wagon trundled off on its eight tall
wheels: away from Smargash, out over the plain

toward the west. Reith, Anacho and Traz sat alone in the aft passenger cubicle.

Anacho was pessimistic in regard to their chances. "The Dirdir will not be confused for long. The difficulties will only make them keen. Do you know that the Dirdir young are like beasts? They must be tamed, then trained and educated. The Dirdir spirit remains feral; hunting is a lust."

"Self-preservation is no less a lust with me," Reith stated.

The sun sank behind the rim; gray-brown dusk settled over the landscape. The wagon paused at a dismal little village; the passengers stretched their legs, drank brackish water raised from a well, haggled for buns with a withered old crone who asked outrageous prices and laughed wildly at counter-proposals.

The wagon proceeded, leaving the old woman muttering beside her tray of buns.

The dusk faded through umber into darkness. From across the wasteland came a weird hooting: the call of night-hounds. In the east rose the pink moon Az, followed presently by blue Braz. Ahead loomed a jut of rock: an ancient volcanic neck, so Reith surmised. From the summit glowed three wan yellow lights. Looking up through his scanscope* Reith saw the ruins of a castle. . . . He dozed for an hour and awoke to find the wagon rolling through soft sand and beside a river. On the opposite bank psillas stood outlined against the moonlit sky. Presently they passed a many-cupolaed manor-house, apparently uninhabited and in the process of decay.

Half an hour later, at midnight, the wagon rumbled into the compound of a large village, to halt for the night. The passengers composed themselves to sleep on their benches or on top of the wagon.

Carina 4269 finally rose: a cool amber disk only gradually dispelling the morning mist. Vendors brought

---

* A binocular photo-multiplying device, with a variable magnification ratio up to 1000 x 1: one of the articles Reith had salvaged from his survival kit.

trays of pickled meats, pastes, strips of boiled bark, toasted pilgrim pod, from which the passengers made a breakfast.

The wagon proceeded to the west toward the Rim Mountains, now jutting high into the sky. Reith occasionally swept the sky with his scanscope but discovered no signs of pursuit.

"Too early yet," said Anacho cheerlessly. "Never fear; it will come."

At noon the wagon reached Siadz, the terminus: a dozen stone huts surrounding a cistern.

To Reith's intense disgust, no transportation, neither motor-wagon nor leap-horse, could be hired for transportation onward across the rim.

"Do you know what lies beyond?" demanded the elder of the village. "The chasms."

"Is there no trail, no trade-route?"

"Who would enter the chasms, for trade or otherwise? What sort of folk are you?"

"Serafs," said Anacho. "We explore for asofa root."

"Ah, the Serafs and their perfumes. I have heard tales. Well, don't play your immortal antics on us; we are a simple people. In any event, there is no asofa among the chasms; only cripthorn, spumet and rackbelly."

"Nevertheless, we will go forth to search."

"Go then. There is said to be an ancient road somewhere to the north, but I know of none who have seen it."

" 'People'? A joke. A few pysantillas, red cors under every rock, bode-birds. If you are extremely unlucky you might meet a fere."

"It seems a dire region."

"Aye, a thousand miles of cataclysm. Still, who knows? Where cowards never venture, heroes find splendor. So it may be with your perfume. Strike out to the north and seek the ancient road to the coast. It will be no more than a mark, a crumble. When darkness comes, make yourself secure: night-hounds range the wastes!"

Reith said, "You have dissuaded us; we will return east with the motor-wagon."

"Wise, wise! Why, after all, throw away your lives, Seraf or no?"

Reith and his companions rode the motor-wagon a mile back down the road, then inconspicuously slid to the ground. The wagon lumbered east and presently disappeared into the amber murk.

There was silence about them. They stood on coarse gray soil, with here and there wisps of salmon-colored thorn and at even greater intervals a coarse tangle of pilgrim plant, which Reith saw with a certain glum satisfaction. "So long as we find pilgrim plant we won't starve."

Traz gave a dubious grunt. "We had best reach the mountains before dark. On the flat night-hounds have advantage over three men."

"I know an even better reason for haste," said Anacho. "The Dirdir won't be puzzled long."

Reith searched the empty sky, the bleak landscape. "They might conceivably become discouraged."

"Never! When thwarted they grow excited, furious with zeal."

"We're not far from the mountains. We can hide in the shadow of the boulders, or in one of the ravines."

An hour's travel brought them under the crumbling basalt palisade. Traz suddenly halted, sniffed the air. Reith could smell nothing, but long since had learned to defer to Traz's perceptions.

"Phung* droppings," said Traz. "About two days old."

Reith nervously checked the availability of his handgun. Eight explosive pellets remained. When these were gone the gun became useless. It might be, thought Reith, that his luck was running out. He asked Traz, "Is it likely to be close at hand?"

Traz shrugged. "The Phung are mad things. For all I know, one stands behind that boulder."

---

* Phung: solitary nocturnal creature indigenous to Tschai.

Reith and Anacho looked uneasily about. Anacho finally said, "Our first concern must be the Dirdir. The critical period has begun. They will have traced us aboard the motor-wagon; they can easily follow us to Siadz. Still, we are not completely without advantage, especially if they lack game-finding instruments."

"What instruments are these?" asked Reith.

"Detectors of human odor or heat radiation. Some trace footprints by residual warmth, others observe exhalations of carbon dioxide and locate a man from a distance of five miles."

"And when they catch their game?"

"The Dirdir are conservative. They do not recognize change," said Anacho. "They need not hunt but are driven by inner forces. They consider themselves beasts of prey, and impose no restraint upon themselves."

"In other words," said Traz, "they will eat us."

Reith was gloomily silent. At last he said, "Well, we must not be captured."

"As Zarfo the Lokhar said, 'Death comes but once.' "

Traz pointed. "Notice the break into the palisade. If ever a road existed, there it must go."

Across barren hummocks of compacted gray soil, around tangles of thorn and tumbled beds of rubble, the three hurried, perspiring and constantly watching the sky. At last they reached the shadow of the notch, but could find no trace of the road. If ever it existed, detritus and erosion had long ago expunged it from view.

Anacho suddenly gave a low sad call. "The sky-car. It comes. We are hunted."

Reith forced back a panicky urge to run. He looked up the notch. A small stream trickled down the center, to terminate in a stagnant tarn. To the right rose a steep slope; to the left, a massive buttress overhung an area of deep shade, at the back of which was an even deeper shadow: the mouth of a cave.

The three crouched behind the tumble which choked half the ravine. Out over the plain the Dirdir boat, with chilling deliberation, slid toward Siadz.

Reith said in a neutral voice, "They can't detect our radiation through the rocks. Our carbon dioxide blows up the notch." He turned to look up the valley.

"No point in running," said Anacho. "There's no sanctuary. If they follow us this far they will chase us forever."

Five minutes later the sky-car returned from Siadz, following the road east, at an altitude of two or three hundred yards. Suddenly is swerved and circled. Anacho said in a fateful voice, "They have found our tracks."

The sky-car came across the plain, directly toward the notch. Reith brought forth his hand-gun. "Eight pellets left. Enough to explode eight Dirdir."

"Not enough to explode one. They carry shields against such missiles."

In another half-minute the sky-car would be overhead. "Best that we take to the cave," said Traz.

"Obviously the haunt of Phung," muttered Anacho. "Or an adit of the Pnume. Let us die cleanly, in the open air."

"We can walk through the pond," said Traz, "and stand below the overhang. Our trail is then broken; they may follow the stream up the valley."

"If we stand here," said Reith, "we're finished for sure."

The three ran through the shallow fringes of the pond, Anacho gingerly bringing up the rear. They huddled under the loom of the cliff. The odor of Phung was strong and rich.

Over the shoulder of the mountain opposite came the sky-boat. "They'll see us!" said Anacho in a hollow voice. "We're in plain sight!"

"Into the cave," hissed Reith. "Back, further back!"

"The Phung—"

"There may be no Phung. The Dirdir are certain!" Reith groped back into the dark, followed by Traz and finally Anacho. The shadow of the sky-car passed over the pond, flitted on up the valley.

Reith flashed his light here and there. They stood in

a large chamber of irregular shape, the far end obscured in murk. Light brown nodules and flakes covered the floor ankle-deep; the walls were crusted over with horny hemispheres, each the size of a man's fist.

"Night-hound larva," muttered Traz.

For a time they stood in silence.

Anacho stole to the cave-mouth, looked cautiously forth. He jerked back. "They've missed our trail; they're circling."

Reith extinguished the light and looked cautiously from the cave-mouth. A hundred yards away the sky-car descended to the ground, silent as a falling leaf. Five Dirdir alighted. For a moment they stood in consultation; then, each carrying a long transparent shield, they advanced into the notch. As if at a signal, two leaped forward like silver leopards, peering along the ground. Two others came behind at a slow lope, weapons ready; the fifth remained to the rear.

The pair in the lead stopped short, communicating in odd squeaks and grunts. "Their hunting language," Anacho muttered, "from the time they were yet beasts."

"They look no different now."

The Dirdir halted at the far shore of the pond. They looked, listened, smelled the air, obviously aware their prey was close at hand.

Reith sighted along his hand-gun, but the Dirdir continually twitched their shields, frustrating his aim.

One of the leading Dirdir searched the valley through binoculars; the other held a black instrument before his eyes. At once he found something of interest. A great bound took him to the spot where Reith, Traz and Anacho had halted before crossing to the cave. Sighting through the black instrument, the Dirdir followed the tracks to the pond, then searched the space below the overhang. He gave a series of grunts and squeaks; the shields jerked about.

Anacho muttered, "They see the cave. They know we're here."

Reith peered into the back reaches of the cave.

Traz said in a matter-of-fact voice, "There is a Phung back there. Or it has not long departed."

"How do you know?"

"I smell it. I feel the pressure."

Reith turned to the Dirdir. Step by step they came, effulgences sparkling up from their heads. Reith spoke in a fateful croak: "Back, into the cave. Perhaps we can set up some kind of ambush."

Anacho gave a stifled groan; Traz said nothing. The three retreated through the dark, across the carpet of brittle granules. Traz touched Reith's arm. He whispered, "Notice the light behind us. The Phung is close at hand."

Reith halted, to strain his eyes into the dark. He saw no light. Silence pressed upon them.

Reith now thought to hear the faintest of scraping sounds. Cautiously he crept back through the dark, gun ready. And now he sensed yellow light: a wavering glimmer reflecting against the cave-wall. The *scrape-scrape-scrape* was somewhat louder. With the utmost caution Reith peered around a jut of rock, into a chamber. A Phung sat, back half-turned, burnishing its brachial plates with a file. An oil lamp emitted a yellow glow; to the side a broad-brimmed black hat and a cloak hung from a peg.

Four Dirdir stood in the mouth of the cave, shields in front, weapons ready; their effulgences, standing high, furnished their only light.

Traz plucked one of the horny hemispheres from the wall. He threw it at the Phung, which gave a startled cluck. Traz pressed Anacho and Reith back behind the jut of rock.

The Phung came forth; they could see its shadow against the glimmer of lamp-light. It returned into its chamber, once more came forth, and now it wore its hat and cloak.

For a moment it stood silent, not four feet from Reith, who thought the creature must surely hear the thud-thud-thud of his heart.

The Dirdir came three bounds forward, effulgences

casting a wan white glow around the chamber. The Phung stood like an eight-foot statue, shrouded in its cloak. It gave a cluck or two of chagrin, then a sudden series of whirling hops took it among the Dirdir. For a taut instant, Dirdir and Phung surveyed each other. The Phung swung out its arms, swept two Dirdir together, squeezing and crushing both. The remaining Dirdir, backing silently away, swung up their weapons. The Phung leaped on them, dashing the weapons aside. It tore the head from one; the other fled, with the Dirdir who had stood guard outside. They ran through the pond; the Phung danced a queer circular jig, sprang forth, leaped ahead of them, kicking water into a spray. It pushed one under the surface and stood on him, while the other ran up the valley. The Phung presently stalked in pursuit.

Reith, Traz and Anacho darted from the cave and made for the sky-car. The surviving Dirdir saw them and gave a despairing scream. The Phung was momentarily distracted; the Dirdir dodged behind a rock, then with desperate speed dashed past the Phung. He seized one of the weapons which had previously been knocked from his hand, and burned off one of the Phung's legs. The Phung fell in a sprawling heap.

Reith, Traz and Anacho were now scrambling into the sky-car; Anacho settled to the controls. The Dirdir screamed a wild admonition, and ran forward. The Phung made a prodigious hop, to alight on the Dirdir with a great flapping of the cloak. With the Dirdir at last a tangle of bones and skin, the Phung hopped to the center of the pond where it stood like a stork, ruefully considering its single leg.

Chapter 3

Below lay the chasms, separated by knife-edged ridges of stone. Black gash paralleled black gash; looking down Reith wondered whether he and his party could possibly have survived to reach the Draschade. Almost certainly not. He speculated: Did the chasms tolerate life of any sort? The old man at Siadz had mentioned pysantillas and fere; who knows what other creatures inhabited the gulches far below? He now noticed, wedged in a crevice high between two peaks, a crumble of angular shapes like an efflorescence from the mother rock: a village, apparently of men, though none could be seen. Where did they find water? In the depths of the chasm? How did they provide themselves with food? Why did they choose so remote an aerie for their home? There were no answers to his questions; the aerie was left behind in the murk.

A voice broke into Reith's musings: a sighing, rasping, sibilant voice, which Reith could not understand.

Anacho touched a button; the voice cut off. Anacho showed no concern; Reith forebore to ask questions.

The afternoon waned; the chasms spread to become flat-bottomed gorges full of darkness, while the intervening ridges showed fringes of dark gold. A region as grim and hopeless as the grave, thought Reith. He recalled the village, now far behind, and became melancholy.

The peaks and ridges ended abruptly to form the front of a gigantic scarp; the floors of the gorges extended and joined. Ahead lay the Draschade. Carina 4269, sinking, laid a topaz trail across the leaden water.

A promontory jutted into the sea, sheltering a dozen

fishing craft, high at bow and stern. A village struggled along the foreshore, lights already glimmering into the dusk.

Anacho circled slowly above the village. He pointed. "Notice the stone building with the two cupolas and the blue lamps? A tavern, or perhaps an inn. I suggest that we put down to refresh ourselves. We have had a most tiring day."

"True, but can the Dirdir trace us?"

"Small risk. They have no means to do so. I long since isolated the identity crystal. And in any event, that is not their way."

Traz peered suspiciously down at the village. Born to the inland steppes, he distrusted the sea and seapeople, considering both uncontrollable and enigmatic. "The villagers may well be hostile, and set upon us."

"I think not," said Anacho in the lofty voice which invariably irritated Traz. "Firstly, we are at the edge of the Wankh realm; these folk will be accustomed to strangers. Secondly, so large an inn implies hospitality. Thirdly, sooner or later we must descend in order to eat and drink. Why not here? The risk can be no greater than at any other inn upon the face of Tschai. Fourthly, we have no plans, no destination. I consider it foolish to fly aimlessly through the night."

Reith laughed. "You have convinced me. Let's go down."

Traz gave his head a sour shake, but put forward no further objections.

Anacho landed the sky-car in a field beside the inn, close under a row of tall black chymax trees which tossed and sighed to a cold wind off the sea. The three alighted warily, but their arrival had attracted no great attention. Two men, hunching along the lane with capes gripped close against the wind, paused a moment to survey the sky-car, then continued with only an idle mutter of comment.

Reassured, the three proceeded to the front of the inn and pushed through a heavy timber door into a great hall. A half-dozen men with sparse sandy hair and pale bland faces stood by the fireplace nursing pewter mugs. They wore rough garments of gray and brown fustian, knee-high boots of well-oiled leather; Reith took them for fishermen. Conversation halted. All turned narrow gazes toward the newcomers. After a moment they reverted to the fire, their mugs, their terse conversations.

A strapping woman in a black gown appeared from a back chamber. "Who be you?"

"Travelers. Can you give us meals and lodging for the night?"

"What's your nature? Are you fjord men? Or Rab?"

"Neither."

"Travelers often be folk who do evil in their own lands and are sent away."

"This is often the case, I agree."

"Mmf. What will you eat?"

"What is to be had?"

"Bread and steamed eel with hilks."

"This then must be our fare."

The woman grunted once more and turned away, but served additionally a salad of sweet lichen and a tray of condiments. The inn, so she informed them, had originally been the residence of the Foglar pirate kings. Treasure was reputedly buried below the dungeons. "But digging only uncovers bones and more bones, some broken, some scorched. Stern men, the Foglars. Well, then, do you wish tea?"

The three went to sit by the fire. Outside the wind roared past the eaves. The landlady came to stoke the blaze. "The chambers are down the hall. If you need women, I must send out; I myself can't serve owing to my sore back, and there will be additional charge."

"Don't trouble in this regard," Reith told her. "So long as the couches are clean we will be content."

"Strange travelers that come in so grand a sky-car. You"—she pointed a finger toward Anacho—"might well be a Dirdirman. Is that a Dirdir sky-car?"

"I might be a Dirdirman and it might be a Dirdir

sky-car. And we might be engaged upon important work where absolute discretion is necessary."

"Aha, indeed!" The woman's jaw slacked. "Something to do with the Wankh, no doubt! Do you know, there's been great changes to the south? The Wankhmen and the Wankh arc all at odds!"

"We are so informed."

The woman leaned forward. "What of the Wankh? Are they in withdrawal? So it is rumored."

"I think not," said Anacho. "While the Dirdir inhabit Haulk, so long will the Wankh hold their Kislovan forts, and the Blue Chasch keep their torpedo pits ready."

The woman cried, "And we, poor miserable humans: pawns of the great folk, never knowing which way to jump! I say Bevol take 'em all, and welcome!"

She shook her fist to south, to southwest and northwest, the directions in which she located her principal antagonists; then she departed the chamber.

Anacho, Traz and Reith sat in the ancient stone hall, watching the fire flicker.

"Well, then," asked Anacho. "What of tomorrow?"

"My plans remain the same," said Reith; "I intend to return to Earth. Somewhere, somehow, I must gain possession of a spaceship. This program is meaningless for you two; you should go where you feel secure: the Isles of Cloud, or perhaps back to Smargash. Wherever you decide, we will go; then perhaps you will allow me to continue in the sky-car."

Anacho's long harlequin face assumed an expression almost prim. "And where will you take yourself?"

"You mentioned the spaceyards at Sivishe; this will be my destination."

"What of money? You will need a great deal, as well as subtlety and, most of all, luck."

"For money there is always the Carabas."

Anacho nodded. "Every desperado of Tschai will tell you the same. But wealth does not come without extreme risk. The Carabas lies within the Dirdir Hunting Preserve; trespassers are fair game. If you evade the Dirdir, there is Buszli the Bandit, the Blue Band, the vampire women, the gamblers, the hook-men. For every man who gains a handful of sequins, another three leave their bones, or fill Dirdir guts."

Reith gave an uneasy grimace. "I'll have to take my chances."

The three sat looking into the fire. Traz stirred. "Once long ago I wore Onmale, and never am I entirely free of the weight. Sometimes I feel it calling from under the soil. In the beginning it ordained life for Adam Reith; now, even if I wished, I would not desert Adam Reith for fear of Onmale."

"I am a fugitive," said Anacho. "I have no life of my own. We have destroyed the first Initiative,* but sooner or later there will be a second Initiative. The Dirdir are pertinacious. Do you know where we might find the most security? At Sivishe, close under the Dirdir city Hei. As for the Carabas . . ." Anacho gave a doleful sigh. "Adam Reith seems to have a knack for survival. I have nothing better to do. I will take my chances."

"I'll say no more," said Reith. "I'm grateful for your company."

For a space the three looked into the flames. Outside the wind whistled and blustered. "Our destination, then, is the Carabas," said Reith. "Why should not the sky-car give us an advantage?"

Anacho fluttered his fingers. "Not in the Black Zone. The Dirdir would take note and instantly be upon us."

"There must be tactics of some sort to lessen the danger," said Reith.

Anacho gave a grim chuckle. "Everyone who visits the Zone has his private theories. Some enter by night; others wear camouflage and puff boots to muffle their tracks. Some organize brigades and march as a unit; others feel more secure alone. Some enter from Zimle;

---

* An inexact rendering of the word *tsau'gsh*: more accurately, a band of determined hunters who have claimed the right to prosecute a quest or a task, in order to win status and reputation.

others come down from Maust. The eventualities are usually the same."

Reith rubbed his chin reflectively. "Do Dirdirmen join the hunt?"

Anacho smiled into the flames. "The Immaculates have been known to hunt. But your concept has no value. Neither you nor Traz nor I could successfully impersonate an Immaculate."

The fire became coals; the three went to their tall dim chambers and slept on hard couches under linens smelling of the sea. In the morning they ate a breakfast of salt biscuit and tea, then settled their tariff and departed the inn.

The day was dreary. Cold tendrils of fog sifted through the chymax trees. The three boarded the sky-car. Up they rose through the overcast, and finally broke out into the wan amber sunlight. Westward they flew, over the Draschade Ocean.

Chapter 4

The gray Draschade rolled below: the ocean which Reith—it seemed an aeon ago—had crossed aboard the cog *Vargaz*. Anacho flew close above the surface, to minimize the risks of detection by Dirdir search-screens. "We have important decisions to make," he announced. "The Dirdir are hunters; we have become prey. In principle, a hunt once initiated must be consummated, but the Dirdir are not a cohesive folk like the Wankh; their programs result from individual initiatives, the so-called *zhna-dih*. This means a great dashing leap, trailing lightning-like sparks. The zeal expended upon finding us depends upon whether the hunt-chief—he who performed the original *zhna-dih*—was aboard the sky-car and is now dead. If so, there is a considerable diminution of risk, unless another Dirdir wishes to assert *h'so*—a word meaning 'marvelous dominance'—and organizes another *tsau'gsh,* whereupon conditions are as before. If the hunt-chief is alive, he becomes our mortal enemy."

Reith asked in wonder, "What was he before?"

Anacho ignored the remark. "The hunt-chief has the force of the community at his disposal, though he asserts his *h'so* more emphatically by *zhna-dih.* However, if he suspects that we fly the sky-car, he might well order up search-screens." Anacho offhandedly indicated a disk of gray glass to the side of the instrument panel. "If we touch a search-screen you'll see a mesh of orange lines."

The hours went by. Anacho somewhat condescendingly explained the operation of the sky-car; both Traz and Reith familiarized themselves with the controls. Carina 4269 swung across the sky, overtaking the sky-car and dropping into the west. The Draschade rolled below, an enigmatic gray-brown waste, blurring and merging into the sky.

Anacho began to talk of the Carabas: "Most sequin-takers enter at Maust, fifty miles south of the First Sea. At Maust are the most complete outfitters' shops, the finest charts and handbooks, and other services. I consider it as good a destination as any."

"Where are the nodes usually found?"

"Anywhere within the Carabas. There is no rule, no system of discovery. Where many folk seek, nodes are naturally few."

"Then why not choose a less popular entry?"

"Maust is popular because it is most convenient."

Reith looked ahead toward the yet unseen coast of Kislovan and the unknown future. "What if we use none of these entries, but some point in between?"

"What is there to gain? The Zone is the same from any direction."

"There must be some way to minimize risks and maximize gains."

Anacho shook his head in disparagement. "You are

a strange and obstinate man! Isn't this attitude a form
of arrogance?"

"No," said Reith. "I don't think so."

"How," argued Anacho, "should you succeed with
such facility where others have failed?"

Reith girnned. "It's not arrogant to wonder why they
failed."

"One of the Dirdir virtues is *zs'hanh,*" said Anacho.
"It means 'contemptuous indifference to the activity of
others.' There are twenty-eight castes of Dirdir, which
I will not enumerate, and four castes of Dirdirmen: the
Immaculates, the Intensives, the Estranes, the Cluts.
Zs'hanh is reckoned an attribute of the fourth through
the thirteenth Dirdir grades. The Immaculates also
practice *zs'hanh.* It is a noble doctrine."

Reith shook his head in wonder. "How have the
Dirdir managed to create and coordinate a technical
civilization? In such a welter of conflicting wills—"

"You misunderstand," said Anacho in his most nasal
voice. "The situation is more complex. To rise in caste
a Dirdir must be accepted into the next highest group.
He wins acceptance by his achievements, not by
causing conflicts. *Zs'hanh* is not always appropriate to
the lower castes, nor for the very highest, which use
the doctrine of *pn'hanh*; 'corrosive or metal-bursting
sagacity.' "

"I must belong in a high caste," said Reith. "I intend to use *pn'hanh* rather than *zs'hanh.* I want to exploit every possible advantage and avoid every risk."

Reith, looking sidewise at the long sour face,
chuckled to himself. *He wants to point out that my
caste is too low for such affectations,* thought Reith,
but he knows that I'll laugh at him.

The sun sank with unnatural deliberation, its rate of
decline slowed by the westward progress of the sky-car.
Toward the end of the afternoon a gray-violet bulk
rose above the horizon, to meet the disk of the pale
brown sun. This was the island Leume, close under the
continent of Kislovan.

Anacho turned the sky-car somewhat to the north

and landed at a dingy village on the sandy north cape.
The three spent the night at the Glass Blower's Inn, a
structure contrived of bottles and jugs discarded by the
shops at the sand-pits behind the town. The inn was
dank and permeated with a peculiar acrid odor; the
evening meal of soup, served in heavy green glass
tureens, evinced something of the same flavor. Reith
remarked on the similarity to Anacho, who summoned
the Gray* servant and put a haughty question. The
servant indicated a large black insect darting across the
floor. "The skarats do indeed be pungent creatures,
and exhale a chife. Bevol made a plague on us, until
we put them to use and found them nutritious. Now we
hardly capture enough."

Reith long had been careful never to make inquiry
regarding foods set before him, but now he looked
askance into the tureen. "You mean . . . the soup?"

"Indeed," declared the servant. "The soup, the
bread, the pickles: all be skarat-flavored, and if we did
not use them of purpose, they'd infest us to the same
effect, so we make a virtue of convenience, and think
to enjoy the taste."

Reith drew back from the soup. Traz ate stolidly.
Anacho gave a petulant sniff and also ate. It occurred
to Reith that never on Tschai had he noticed squeam-
ishness. He heaved a deep sigh, and since no other
food was forthcoming, swallowed the rancid soup.

In the dim brown morning breakfast was again soup,
with a garnish of sea vegetables. The three departed
immediately after, flying northwest across Leume Gulf
and the stony wastes of Kislovan.

Anacho, usually nerveless, now became edgy,
searching the sky, peering down at the ground, scruti-
nizing the knobs and bubbles, the patches of brown fur
and vermilion velvet, the quivering mirrors which
served as instruments. "We approach the Dirdir

---

* Gray: Loose term for the various peoples hybridized of
Dirdirmen, Marshmen, Chaschmen and others, generally
stocky and large-headed, often with yellow-gray complexions,
occasionally somewhat albinoid.

realm," he said. "We will veer north to the First Sea, then bear west to Khorai, where we must leave the sky-car and travel the Zoga'ar zum Fulkash am* to Maust. Then . . . the Carabas."

Chapter 5

Over the great Stone Desert flew the sky-car, parallel to the black and red peaks of the Zopal Range, over parched dust-flats, fields of broken rock, dunes of dark pink sand, a single oasis surrounded by plumes of white smoke-tree.

Late in the afternoon a windstorm drove lion-colored rolls of dust across the landscape, submerging Carina 4269 in murk. Anacho swung the sky-car north. Presently a black-blue line on the horizon indicated the First Sea.

Anacho immediately landed the sky-car upon the barrens, some ten miles short of the sea.

"Khorai is yet hours ahead; best not to arrive after dark. The Khors are a suspicious folk, and flourish their knives at a harsh word. At night they strike without provocation."

"These are the folk who will guard our sky-car?"

"What thief would be mad enough to trouble the Khors?"

Reith looked around the waste. "I prefer supper at the Glass Blower's Inn to nothing whatever."

"Ha!" said Anacho. "In the Carabas you will recall the silence and peace of this night with longing."

The three bedded themselves down into the sand. The night was dark and brilliantly clear. Directly overhead burned the constellation Clari, within which, un-

---

* Literally: the way of death's-heads with purple-gleaming eye sockets.

seen to the eye, glimmered the Sun. Would he ever again see Earth? Reith wondered. How often then would he lie under the night sky looking up into Argo Navis for the invisible brown sun Carina 4269 and its dim planet Tschai?

A flicker inside the sky-car attracted his attention: he went to look and found a mesh of orange lines wavering across the radar screen.

Five minutes later it disappeared, leaving Reith with a sense of chill and desolation.

In the morning the sun rose at the edge of the flat plain in a sky uncharacteristically clear and transparent, so that each small irregularity, each pebble, left a long black shadow. Taking the sky-car into the air, Anacho flew low to the ground; he too had noticed the orange flicker of the night before. The waste became less forbidding: clumps of stunted smoke-tree appeared, and presently black dendron and bladder-bush.

They reached the First Sea and swung west, following the shoreline. They passed over villages: huddles of dull brown brick with conical roofs of black iron, beside copses of enormous dyan trees, which Anacho declared to be sacred groves. Rickety piers like dead centipedes sprawled out into the dark water; double-ended boats of black wood were drawn up the beach. Looking through the scanscope Reith noted men and women with mustard-yellow skins. They wore black gowns and tall black hats; as the sky-car passed over they looked up without friendliness.

"Khors," stated Anacho. "Strange folk with secret ways. They are different by day and by night—at least this is the report. Each individual owns two souls which come and go with dawn and sunset, so that each is two different persons. Peculiar tales are told." He pointed ahead. "Notice the shore, where it draws back into a funnel."

Reith, looking in the direction indicated, saw one of the now-familiar dyan copses and a huddle of dull brown huts with black iron roofs. From a small com-

pound a road led south over the rolling hills toward the
Carabas.

Anacho said, "Behold the sacred grove of the Khors,
in which, so it is said, souls are exchanged. Yonder you
see the caravan terminus and the road to Maust. I dare
not take the sky-car further; hence we must land and
make our way to Maust as ordinary sequin-takers
which is not necessarily a disadvantage."

"And when we return will the sky-car still be here?"

Anacho pointed down to the harbor. "Notice the
boats at anchor."

Looking through his scanscope Reith observed three
or four dozen boats of every description.

"Those boats," said Anacho, "brought sequin-takers
to Khorai from Coad, Hedaijha, the Low Isles, from
the Second Sea and the Third Sea. If the owners return
within a year, they sail from Khorai and to their
homes. If within the year they do not return, the boat
becomes the property of the harbor-master. No doubt
we can arrange the same contract."

Reith made no arguments against the scheme, and
Anacho dropped the sky-car toward the beach.

"Remember," Anacho warned, "the Khors are a
sensitive people. Do not speak to them; pay them no
heed except from necessity, in which case you must use
the fewest possible words. They consider garrulity a
crime against nature. Do not stand upwind of a Khor,
nor if possible downwind; such acts are symbolic of
antagonism. Never acknowledge the presence of a
woman; do not look toward their children—they will
suspect you of laying a curse; and above all ignore the
sacred grove. Their weapon is the iron dart which they
throw with astonishing accuracy; they are a dangerous
people."

"I hope I remember everything," said Reith.

The sky-car landed upon the dry shingle; seconds
later a great gaunt brown-skinned man, with deep-sunk
eyes, concave cheeks, a crag of a nose, came running
forward, his coarse brown smock flapping. "Are you
for the Carabas, the dreadful Carabas?"

Reith gave a cautious assent: "This is our design."

"Sell me your sky-car! Four times I have entered the Zone, creeping from rock to rock; now I have my sequins. Sell me your sky-car, so that I may return to Holangar."

"Unfortunately we will need the sky-car upon our return," said Reith.

"I offer you sequins, purple sequins!"

"They mean nothing to us; we go to find sequins of our own."

The gaunt man gave a gesture of emotion too wild to be expressed in words and lunged off down the beach. A pair of Khors now approached: men somewhat slender and delicate of physique, wearing black gowns and cylindrical black hats which gave the illusion of height. The mustard-yellow faces were grave and still, the noses thin and small, the ears fragile shells. Fine black hair grew up rather than down, to be contained within the tall hat. They seemed to Reith a stream of humanity as divergent as the Chasch-men— perhaps a distinct species.

The older of the two spoke in a thin soft voice: "Why are you here?"

"We go to take sequins," said Anacho. "We hope to leave the sky-car in your care."

"You must pay. The sky-car is a valuable device."

"So much the better for you should we fail to return, We can pay nothing."

"If you return, you must pay."

"No, no payment. Do not insist or we will fly directly to Maust."

The mustard-yellow faces showed no quiver of emotion. "Very well, but we allow you only to the month Temas."

"Only three months? Too short a period! Give us until the end of Meumas, or better Azaimas."

"Until Meumas. Your sky-car will be secure against all but those from whom you stole it."

"It will be totally secure; we are not thieves."

"So be it. Until the first day of Meumas, on the precise instant."

The three took their possessions and walked through Khorai to the caravan terminus. Under an open shed a motor wagon was being prepared for a journey, with a dozen men of as many races standing by. The three made arrangements for passage, and an hour later departed Khorai, along the road south to Maust.

Over barren hills and dry swales rolled the motor wagon, halting for the night at a hostel operated by an order of white-faced women. They were either members of an orgiastic religious sect or simple prostitutes; long after Reith, Anacho and Traz had stretched out upon the benches which served as beds, drunken shouts and wild laughter came from the smoky common room.

In the morning the common room was dim and quiet, reeking with spilled wine and the smoke of dead lamps. Men huddled face-down over tables, or sprawled along benches, their faces the color of ash. The women of the place entered, now harsh-voiced and peremptory, with cauldrons of thin yellow goulash. The men stirred and groaned, somberly ate from earthenware bowls and staggered out to the motor wagon, which presently set forth to the south.

By noon Maust appeared in the distance: a jumble of tall narrow buildings with high gables and crooked roof-lines, built of dark timber and age-blackened tile. Beyond, a barren plain extended to the dim Hills of Recall. Running boys came out to meet the motor wagon. They shouted slogans and held up signs and banners: "Sequin-takers attention! Kobo Hux will sell one of his excellent sequin-detectors." "Formulate your plans at the Inn of Purple Lights." "Weapons, puff-pads, maps, digging implements from Sag the Mercantilist are eminently useful." "Do not grope at random; the Seer Garzu divines the location of large purple nodes." "Flee the Dirdir with all possible agility; use supple boots provided by Awalko." "Your last thoughts will be pleasant if, before death, you first consume the euphoric tablets formulated by Laus the Thaumaturge." "Enjoy a jolly respite before entering the Zone at the Platform of Merriment."

The motor wagon halted in a compound at the edge of Maust. The passengers alighted into a crowd of bawling men, urgent boys, grimacing girls, each with a new proffer. Reith, Traz and Anacho pushed through the throng avoiding as best they could the hands which reached to grasp them and their possessions.

They entered a narrow street running between tall, age-darkened structures, the beer-colored sunlight barely penetrating to the street. Certain of the houses sold gear and implements conceivably useful to the sequin-taker: grading kits, camouflage, spoor eliminators, tongs, forks, bars, monoculars, maps, guides, talismans and prayer powders. From other houses came the clash of cymbals, a raucous honking of oboes, accompanied by calls of drunken exaltation. Certain of the buildings catered to gamblers; others functioned as inns, with restaurants occupying the ground floor. Everywhere lay the weight of antiquity, even to the dry aromatic odor of the air. Stones had been polished by the casual touch of hands; interior timbers were dark and waxy; the old brown tiles showed a subtle luster to glancing light.

At the back of the central plaza stood a spacious hostelry, which appeared to offer comfortable accommodations and which Anacho favored, though Traz grumbled at what he considered excessive and unnecessary luxury. "Must we pay the price of a leap-horse merely to sleep the night?" he complained. "We have passed a dozen inns more to my taste."

"In due course you will learn to appreciate the civilized niceties," said Anacho indulgently. "Come, let us see what is offered within."

Through a portal of carved wood they entered the foyer. Chandeliers fashioned to represent sequin-clusters hung from the ceiling; a magnificent rug, black of field with a taupe border and five starbursts of scarlet and ocher, cushioned the tile floor.

A major domo approached to inquire their needs. Anacho spoke for three chambers, clean linen, baths and unguents. "And what do you demand in the way of tariff?"

"For such accommodation each must pay a hundred sequins* per day," replied the major domo.

Traz gave an exclamation of shock; even Anacho was moved to protest. "What?" he exclaimed. "For three modest chambers, you demand three hundred sequins? Have you no sense of proportion? The charges are outrageous."

The major domo gave his head a curt inclination. "Sir, this is the famous Alawan Inn, at the threshold of the Carabas. Our patrons never begrudge themselves; they go forth either for wealth or the experience of a Dirdir intestine. What then a few sequins more or less? If you are unable to pay our fees I suggest the Den of Restful Repose of the Black Zone Inn. Notice, however, that the tariff includes access to a buffet of good-quality victuals as well as a library of charts, guides and technical advice, not to mention the services of an expert consultant."

"All very well," said Reith. "First we will look into the Black Zone Inn, and one or two other establishments."

The Black Zone Inn occupied the loft above a gambling establishment. The Den of Restful Repose was a cold barracks a hundred yards north of town, beside a refuse dump.

After inspecting several other hospices the three returned to the Alawan, where by dint of furious haggling they managed to secure a somewhat lower rate, which they were forced to pay in advance.

After a meal of stewed hackrod and mealcake, the three repaired to the library, at the back of the second floor. The side wall displayed a great map of the Zone; shelves held pamphlets, portfolios, compilations. The consultant, a small sad-eyed man, sat to the side and

---

* Sums expressed in sequins are in terms of the unit value sequin, the "clear."

responded to questions in a confidential whisper. The three passed the afternoon studying the physiography of the Zone, the tracks of successful and unsuccessful ventures, the statistical distribution of Dirdir kills. Of those who entered the Zone, something under two-thirds returned, with an average gain of sequins to the value of about six hundred. "The figures here are somewhat misleading," Anacho stated. "They include the fringe-runners who never venture more than half a mile into the Zone. The takers who work the hills and the far slopes account for most of the deaths and most of the wealth."

There were a thousand aspects to the science of sequin-taking, with arrays of statistics to illuminate every possible inquiry. Upon sighting a Dirdir band a sequin-taker might run, hide or fight with chances of clean escape calculated in terms of physiography, the time of day, proximity to the Portal of Gleams. Takers organized into bands for self-protection attracted an overcompensating number of Dirdir and their chances of survival decreased. Nodes were found in all parts of the Zone, most being found in the Hills of Recall and upon the South Stage, the savanna at the far side of the hills. The Carabas were reckoned no-man's land, takers occasionally ambushing each other; such acts were reckoned as eleven percent of the risk.

Dusk approached, and the library became filled with gloom. The three went down to the refectory, where, under the light of three great chandeliers, servitors in black silk livery had already laid out the evening meal. Reith was moved to remark at so much elegance, to which Anacho gave a bark of sardonic amusement. "How else to justify such exorbitant tariffs?" He went off to the buffet and returned with three cups of spiced wine.

The three, leaning back in the ancient settees, observed the other sojourners, most of whom sat alone. A few were in pairs, and a single group of four huddled at a far table, in dark cloaks and hoods which revealed only long ivory noses.

Anacho spoke: "Eighteen men in the room, with ourselves. Nine will find sequins, nine will find none. Two may locate a node of high value, purple or scarlet. Ten, perhaps twelve, will pass through Dirdir guts. Six, or perhaps eight, will return to Maust. Those ranging the farthest to find the choicest nodes run the most risk; the six or eight will show no great profit."

Traz said dourly, "Every day in the Zone a man faces one chance in four of death. His average gain is about four hundred sequins: it would seem that these men, and ourselves as well, value life at only sixteen hundred sequins."

"Somehow we've got to change the odds," said Reith.

"Everyone who comes to the Zone makes similar plans," said Anacho dryly. "Not all succeed."

"Then we must try something no one else has considered."

Anacho made a skeptical sound.

The three went forth to explore the town. The music houses showed red and green lights; on the balconies frozen-faced girls twitched and postured and sang strange soft songs. The gambling houses showed brighter lights and more fervent activity. Each seemed to specialize in a particular game, as simple as the throw of fourteen-faced dice, as complex as chess played against the house professionals.

They stopped to watch a game called Locate the Prime Purple Node. A board thirty feet long by ten feet wide represented the Carabas. The Forelands, the Hills of Recall, the South Stage, the gorges and valleys, the savannas, the streams and forests were faithfully depicted. Blue, red and purple lights indicated the location of nodes, sparse along the Forelands, more plentiful in the Hills of Recall and on the South Stage. Khusz, the Dirdir hunting camp, was a white block, with purple prongs rising from each corner. A numbered grid was superimposed upon all. A dozen players overlooked the board, each controlling a manikin. Also on the board were the effigies of four lunging Dirdir hunters. The players in turn cast fourteen-sided dice to determine the movement of all the manikins across the grid, as each player elected. The Dirdir hunters, moving to the same numbers, endeavored to cross an intersection on which rested a manikin, whereupon the manikin was declared destroyed and removed from the game. Each manikin sought to cross the lights representing sequin nodes, thus augmenting his score. Whenever he chose, he left the Zone by the Portal of Gleams and was paid his winnings. More often, prompted by greed, the player held his manikin on the board until a Dirdir struck it down, by which he lost the totality of his gain. Reith watched the game in fascination. The players sat clenching the rails of their booths. They stared and fidgeted, calling hoarse orders to the operators, yelling in exultation when they won a node, groaning at the approach of the Dirdir, leaning back with sick faces when their manikins were destroyed and their winnings lost.

The game ended. No further manikins roamed the Carabas.

No Dirdir hunted an empty Zone. The players stiffly descended from their booths; those who had won free of the Zone took their winnings. The Dirdir returned to Khusz beyond the South Stage. New players bought manikins, climbed into the booths and the game began once more.

Reith, Traz and Anacho continued along the street. Reith paused at a booth to scan packets of folded paper on display. Placards read:

Meticulously annotated across seventeen years: the chart of Sanbour Yan, for a mere 1,000 sequins, guaranteed to be unexploited.

and

The chart of Goragonso the Mysterious, who lived in the Zone like a shadow, nurturing his secret nodes like children, at a mere 3500 sequins. Never exploited.

Reith looked to Anacho for explanation.

"Simple enough. Such folk as Sabour Yan and Gora-gonso the Mysterious over the years explore the safer regions of the Carabas, seeking out low-grade nodes, the waters and milks, the pale blues which are known as sards, the pale greens. When they locate such nodes they carefully note their position and conceal them as best they may, under heaps of gravel or slabs of shale, thinking to return in later years after the nodes mature. If they find purple nodes so much the better, but in the near regions which for safety's sake they frequent, purple nodes are few—save those which as 'waters' or 'milks' or 'sards,' were discovered and concealed a gen-eration before. When such men are killed, their charts become valuable documents. Unfortunately, buying such a chart can be risky. The first person to come into possession of the chart might 'exploit' it, removing the choicest nodes, and then putting the chart up for sale as 'unexploited.' Who can prove otherwise?"

The three returned to the Alawan. In the foyer a single chandelier exuded the light of a hundred sullen jewels, which lost itself in the shadows, with only a colored gleam here and there on the dark wood. The refectory was also dim, occupied by a few murmuring groups. From an urn they drew bowls of pepper-tea and settled themselves in a booth.

Traz spoke in a disgruntled voice: "This place is in-sane: Maust and the Carabas together. We should leave and seek wealth in some normal manner."

Anacho gave an airy wave of white fingers and spoke in a didactic and fluting voice: "Maust is merely an aspect of the interplay between men and money, and must be viewed on this basis."

"Must you always talk gibberish?" demanded Traz. "To gain sequins either in Maust or in the Zone is a gamble, at poor odds. I do not care to gamble."

"As far as I am concerned," said Reith, "I plan to gain sequins, but I do not intend to gamble."

"Impossible!" Anacho declared. "In Maust you

gamble with sequins; in the Zone you gamble with your life. How can you avoid doing so?"

"I can try to reduce the odds to a tolerable level."

"Everyone hopes to do the same. But Dirdir fires burn nightly across the Carabas, and at Maust the shopkeepers earn more than most sequin-takers."

"Taking sequins is uncertain and slow," said Reith. "I prefer sequins already gathered."

Anacho pursed his lips in quizzical calculation. "You plan to rob the sequin-gatherers? The process is risky."

Reith looked up at the ceiling. How could Anacho still misread the processes of his mind? "I plan to rob no sequin-takers."

"Then I am puzzled," said Anacho. "Whom do you intend to rob?"

Reith spoke with care. "While we watched the hunting game, I began to wonder: when Dirdir kill a taker, what happens to his sequins?"

Anacho gave his fingers a bored flutter. "The sequins are booty; what else?"

"Consider a typical Dirdir hunt-party: how long will it remain in the Zone?"

"Three to six days. Grand hunts and commemoratives are longer; competition hunts are somewhat less extended."

"And, in a day, how many kills will a typical party make?"

Anacho considered. "Each hunter naturally hopes for a trophy each day out. The usual well-seasoned party kills two or three times each day, sometimes more. They waste much meat, necessarily."

"So that the typical hunting party returns to Khusz with sequins from as many as twenty takers."

Anacho said curtly, "So it might be."

"The average taker carries sequins to the value of, let us say, five hundred. Hence each hunting party returns with a value of ten thousand sequins."

"Don't allow the calculation to excite you," Anacho

remarked in the dryest of voices. "The Dirdir are not a generous folk."

"The game-board, I take it, is an accurate representation of the Zone?"

Anacho gave a dour nod. "Reasonably so. Why do you ask?"

"Tomorrow I want to trace the hunt routes out from Khusz and back again. If the Dirdir come to the Carabas to hunt men, they can hardly protest if men hunt Dirdir."

"Who can imagine men hunting the Effulgents?" croaked Anacho.

"It's never been done before?"

"Never! Do gekkos hunt smur?"

"In this case we gain the benefit of surprise."

"No doubt of that!" declared Anacho. "But you must proceed without me; I will have none of it."

Traz choked back a guffaw; Anacho swung about. "What amuses you?"

"Your fear."

Anacho leaned back in his seat. "If you knew the Dirdir as I do, you would fear too."

"They are alive. Kill, they die."

"They are hard to kill. When they hunt, they use a separate region of their mind, what they call the 'Old State.' No man can stand against them. Reith's concept verges upon insanity."

"Tomorrow we'll study the hunt-board again," said Reith in a soothing voice. "Something may suggest itself."

Chapter 6

Three days later, an hour before dawn, Reith, Traz and Anacho departed Maust. Passing through the Portal of Gleams, they set out across the Foreland toward

the Hills of Recall, black on the mottled dark brown
and violet sky, ten miles to the south. Ahead and behind, a dozen other shapes ran half-crouched through
the cool gloom. Some had burdened themselves with
equipment: digging implements, graders, weapons, de-
odorizing ointment, face-stains, camouflage; others
had no more than a sack, a knife, a wad of alimentary
paste.

Carina 4269 shouldered up through the murk, and
some of the takers, crawling into patches of scrub,
concealed themselves under camouflage cloth, to await
the coming of dusk before proceeding further. Others
plunged ahead, anxious to reach the Boulder Patch, ac-
cepting the risk of interception. Stimulated by evidence
of this risk—ashes mingled with burned bones and
scraps of leather—Reith, Traz and Anacho accelerated
their pace. Half-trotting, half-running, they gained the
haven of the Boulder Patch, where Dirdir did not care
to hunt, without untoward incident.

They put down their packs, and stretched out to
rest. Almost at once a pair of hulking figures drew
near: men of no race identifiable to Reith, brown of
skin with long tangled black hair and curly beards.
They wore rags; they stank abominably and inspected
the three with truculent assurance. "We are in com-
mand of these premises," groaned one in a gutteral
voice. "Your cost for respite is five sequins each; if you
refuse we will thrust you into the open, and notice!
Dirdir stalk the northern ridge."

Anacho instantly leaped to his feet and with his
shovel struck the speaker a great blow on the head.
The second man swung his cudgel; Anacho cut up with
his shovel blade, catching the man a maiming blow under the wrists. The cudgel flew aside; the man tottered
back, looking in horror at his hands. They flapped under his wrists like a pair of empty gloves. Anacho said,
"Go forth yourself to face the Dirdir." He jumped
foward with shovel raised; the two shambled off into
the rocks. Anacho watched them go. "We had better
move."

The three took their packs and started away; almost as they did so a great chunk of rock flew down to smash into the ground. Traz jumped up on a boulder and fired his catapult, evoking a wail of distress.

The three took themselves a hundred yards south, somewhat up the slope from the Boulder Patch, where they commanded a view across the Forelands and yet could not easily be approached from the rear.

Settling back, Reith brought out his scanscope and studied the landscape. He discerned half a dozen furtive takers, and a band of Dirdir on a promontory to the east. For ten minutes the Dirdir stood immobile, then suddenly disappeared. A moment later he picked them out again, moving with long lunging strides down the slope and out upon the Forelands.

During the afternoon, with no Dirdir in view, takers began to venture from the Boulder Patch. Reith, Traz and Anacho climbed the slope, making for the ridge as directly as caution permitted. They were now alone. Not a sound could be heard.

What with the need for stealth, progress was slow; sunset found them toiling up a gulch just below the ridge, and they came forth just in time to see the last corroded sliver of Carina 4269 fade from sight. To the south the ground sloped in long rolls and swales down to the Stage: rich ground for sequins, but highly dangerous owing to the proximity of Khusz, about ten miles to the south.

With twilight a curious mood, mixed of melancholy and horror, settled over the Carabas. In all directions winking fires appeared, each with its macabre implication. Amazing, thought Reith, that men, for any inducement whatever, would enter such a place. No more than a quarter-mile distant a fire sprang into existence, and the three quickly crouched into the shadows. The pale shapes of the Dirdir were clear to the naked eye.

Reith studied them through the scanscope. They stalked back and forth, their effulgences streaming like long phosphorescent antennae, and they seemed to be emitting sounds too soft to be heard.

Anacho whispered, "They use the 'Old State' of their brains; they are truly wild beasts, just as on the Sibol plains a million years ago."

"Why do they walk back and forth?"

"It is their custom; they ready themselves for their feeding frenzy."

Reith scrutinized the ground around the fire. In the shadows lay two heaving shapes. "They're alive!" whispered Reith in dismay.

Anacho grunted. "The Dirdir don't care to carry burdens. The prey must run alongside, hopping and leaping like the Dirdir—all day if need be. If the prey flags, they sting him with nerve-fire and he runs with greater agility."

Reith put down the scanscope.

Anacho spoke in a voice carefully toneless: "You see them now in the 'Old State,' as wild beasts, which is their elemental nature. They are magnificent. In other cases they show magnificence of a different sort. Men cannot judge them, but merely stand back in awe."

"What of the elite Dirdirmen?"

"The Immaculates? What of them?"

"Do they imitate the Dirdir at hunting?"

Anacho looked off over the dark Zone. In the east a pink flush heralded the rising of the moon Az. "The Immaculates hunt. Naturally they cannot match Dirdir fervor and they are not privileged to hunt the Zone." He glanced toward the nearby fire. "In the morning the wind will blow from us to them. Best that we move on through the dark."

Az, low in the sky, cast a pink sheen over the landscape; Reith could think only of watered blood. They moved east and south, picking a painful way across the rocky bones of old Tschai. The Dirdir fire receded and passed from sight behind a bluff. For a period the three descended toward the Stage. They halted to sleep a fitful few hours, then once more continued down through the Hills of Recall. Az now hung low in the west, while

Braz lifted into the east. The night was clear; every object showed a double pink and blue shadow.

Traz went into the lead, watching, listening, testing each step. Two hours before dawn he stopped short and motioned his comrades to stillness. "Dead smoke," he whispered. "A camp ahead . . . something is stirring."

The three listened. The landscape gave back only silence. Moving with utmost stealth, Traz angled away on a new route, up over a ridge, down through a copse of feather-fronds. Once more halting to listen, Traz suddenly gestured the other two back into deep shade. From concealment they saw on the brow of the hill a pair of pale shapes, which stood silent and alert for ten minutes, then abruptly vanished.

Reith whispered, "Did they know we were near?"

"I don't think so," Traz muttered. "Still, they might have picked up our scent."

Half an hour later they went cautiously forward, keeping to the shadows. Dawn colored the east; Az was gone, followed by Braz. The three hurried through plum-colored gloom, and finally took shelter in a dense clump of torquil. At sunrise, among the litter of twigs and curled black leaves, Traz found a node the size of his two fists. When cracked loose from its brittle stem and split, hundreds of sequins spilled forth, each glowing with a point of scarlet fire.

"Beautiful!" whispered Anacho. "Enough to excite avidity! A few more finds like this and we could abandon Adam Reith's insane plan."

They searched further through the copse, but found nothing more.

Daylight revealed the South Stage savanna stretching east and west into the haze of distance. Reith studied his map, comparing the mountain behind with the depicted relief. "Here we are." He touched down his finger. "The Dirdir returning to Khusz pass yonder, west of the Boundary Woods, which is our destination."

"No doubt our destiny as well," remarked Anacho with a pessimistic sniff.

"I would as soon die killing Dirdir as any other way," said Traz.

"One does not die killing Dirdir," Anacho corrected him delicately. "They do not permit it. Should someone make the attempt they prickle him with nerve-fire."

"We'll do our best," said Reith. Lifting the scan-scope he searched the landscape and along the ridge discovered three Dirdir hunting parties, scanning the slopes for game. A wonder, thought Reith, that any men whatever survived to return to Maust.

The day passed slowly. Traz and Anacho searched under the scrub for nodes, without success. During the middle afternoon a hunt crossed the slope not half a mile distant. First came a man bounding like a deer, his legs extending mightily forward and back. Fifty yards behind ran three Dirdir without exertion. The fugitive, despairing, halted with his back to a rock and prepared to fight; he was swarmed upon and over-whelmed. The Dirdir crouched over the prostrate form, performed some sort of manipulation, then stood erect. The man lay twitching and thrashing. "Nerve-fire," said Anacho. "Somehow he annoyed them, perhaps by carrying an energy weapon." The Dirdir trooped away. The victim, by a series of grotesque efforts, gained his feet, and started a lurching flight toward the hills. The Dirdir paused, looked after him. The man halted and gave a great cry of anguish. He turned and followed the Dirdir. They began to run, bounding in feral ex-uberance. Behind, running with crazy abandon, came their captive. The group disappeared to the north.

Anacho said to Reith, "You intend to pursue your plans?"

Reith felt a sudden yearning to be out of the Cara-bas, as far away as possible. "I understand why the plan hasn't been tried before."

Afternoon faded into a sad and gentle evening. As soon as fires appeared along the hillsides, the three de-parted their covert and set off to the north.

At midnight they reached the Boundary Wood. Traz, fearing the sinuous half-reptilian beast known as the smur, was reluctant to enter. Reith made no argument and the three kept to the fringe of the forest until dawn.

With the coming of light they performed a cautious exploration, and found nothing more noxious than fluke lizards. From the western edge of the woods Khusz was clearly visible, only three miles south; entering and leaving the Zone the Dirdir skirted the forest.

In the afternoon, after careful assessment of all the potentialities of the woods, the three set to work. Traz dug, Anacho and Reith worked to fabricate a great rectangular net, using twigs, branches and the cord they had brought in their packs.

On the evening of the following day the apparatus was complete. Surveying the system Reith alternated between hope and despair. Would the Dirdir react as he hoped they might? Anacho seemed to think so, though he spoke much of nerve-fire and exhibited intense pessimism.

Middle morning and early afternoon, when the hunts returned to Khusz, were theoretically the productive periods. Earlier and later the Dirdir tended to go forth; the attention of these groups the three did not care to attract.

The night passed and the sun rose on a day which one way or another must prove to be fateful. For a time it seemed that rain would fall, but by midmorning the clouds had drifted south; in the suddenly clear air the light of Carina 4269 was like an antique tincture.

Reith waited at the edge of the woods, sweeping the landscape through his scanscope. To the north appeared a party of four dirdir loping easily along the trail to Khusz. "Here they come," said Reith. "This is it."

The Dirdir came bounding down the trail, giving occasional whistles of exuberance. Hunting had been good; they had enjoyed themselves. But look! What was there? A man-beast at the edge of the forest! What did the fool do here so close to Khusz? The Dirdir sprang in happy pursuit.

The man-beast ran for his life, as did all such creatures. It faltered early and stood at bay, back to a tree. Venting their horrifying death-cry the Dirdir lunged forward. Under the feet of the foremost the ground gave way; he dropped out of sight. The remaining three halted in amazement. A sound: a crackle, a thrash; on top of them fell a mat of twigs, under which they were trapped. And here came men, unspeakably triumphant! A ruse, a ploy! With rage tearing their viscera, they struggled vainly against the mat, desperately intent to win free, to submerge the wicked men in hate and horror. . . .

The Dirdir were killed, by stabbing, hewing and blows of the shovel.

The mat was raised, the bodies stripped of sequins and dragged away, the deadfall repaired.

A second group came down from the north: only three, but creatures resplendent in casques, with effulgences like incandescent wires. Anacho spoke in awe: "These are Hundred-Trophy Excellences!"

"So much the better." Reith signaled to Traz. "Bring them in; we'll teach them excellence."

Traz behaved as before, showing himself, then fleeing as if in panic. The Excellences pursued without vehemence; they had enjoyed a fruitful hunt. The way under the dendrons had been trodden before, perhaps by other hunters. The quarry, curiously enough, showed little of the frantic agility which added zest to the hunt; in fact, he had turned to face them, his back to an enormous gnarled torquil. Fantastic! He waved a blade. Did he challenge them, the Excellences? Launch forward, leap on him, rend him to the ground, with the trophy to the first to touch him! But—shock!—the ground collapsing, the forest falling; a delirium of confusion! And look: submen coming forth with blades, to hack, to stab! Mind-bursting rage, a frenzy of struggle, hissing and screaming—then the blade.

There were four slaughters that day, four on the next, five on the third day, by which time the process had become an efficient routine. During mornings and evenings the bodies were buried and the gear repaired. The business seemed as passionless as fishing—until Reith recalled the hunts he had witnessed and so restored his zeal.

The decision to halt the operation derived not from the diminution of profit—each party of hunters carried booty to a value of as much as twenty thousand sequins—or any lessening of fervor on the part of the three. But even after sorting out the clears, milks and sards the booty was an almost unmanageable bulk, and Anacho's pessimism had become apprehension. "Sooner or later the parties will be missed. There will be a search; how could we escape?"

"One more kill," said Traz. "Here now comes a group, rich from their hunting."

"But why? We have all the sequins we can carry!"

"We can discard our sards and some emeralds, and carry only reds and purples."

Anacho looked at Reith, who shrugged. "One more band."

Traz went to the edge of the forest and performed his now well-schooled simulation of panic. The Dirdir failed to react. Had they seen him? They advanced with no acceleration of pace. Traz hesitated a moment, then once again showed himself. The Dirdir saw him; apparently they had also seen him on the first occcasion, for instead of leaping into immediate pursuit they continued their easy jog. Watching from the shadows, Reith tried to decide whether they were suspicious or merely sated with hunting.

The Dirdir halted to examine the track into the forest. They came into the wood slowly, one in the lead, another behind, two holding up the rear. Reith faded back to his post.

"Trouble," he told Anacho. "We may have to fight our way out."

" 'Fight'?" cried Anacho. "Four Dirdir, three men?"

Traz, a hundred yards down the trail, decided to stimulate the Dirdir. Stepping into the open, he aimed his catapult at the foremost and fired a bolt into the creature's chest. It gave a whistle of outrage and sprang forward, effulgences stiff and furiously bright.

Traz dodged back, went to stand in his usual spot, a grin of irrational pleasure on his face. He brandished his blade. The wounded Dirdir charged, and crashed into the pitfall. Its yells became a weird keening of shock and pain. The remaining three stopped short, then came balefully forward, step by step. Reith pulled the net release; it dropped, capturing two; one danced back.

Reith came forth. He yelled to Anacho and Traz, "Kill those under the net!" He jumped through the tangle to confront the remaining Dirdir. Under no circumstances must it escape.

Escape was remote from its mind. It sprang upon Reith like a leopard, ripping with its talons. Traz ran forward brandishing his dagger and threw himself on the Dirdir's back. The Dirdir rolled over backward, and tearing Traz's legs loose, made play with his own dagger. Anacho leaped forward; with one mighty swordstroke he hacked apart the Dirdir's arm; with a second blow he clove the creature's head. Staggering and tottering, cursing and panting, the three finished off the remaining Dirdir, then stood in vast relief that they had fared so well. Blood pumped from Traz's leg. Reith applied a tourniquet, opened the first-aid kit he had brought with him to Tschai. He disinfected the wound, applied a toner, pressed the wound together, sprayed on a film of synthetic skin, and eased off the tourniquet. Traz grimaced, but made no complaint. Reith brought forth a pill. "Swallow this. Can you stand?"

Traz stiffly rose to his feet.

"Can you walk?"

"Not too well."

"Try to keep moving, to prevent the leg from going stiff."

Reith and Anacho searched the corpses for booty, to their enormous profit: a purple node, two scarlets, a deep blue, three pale greens and two pale blues. Reith shook his head in marvel and vexation. "Wealth! But useless unless we get it back to Maust."

He watched Traz limping back and forth with obvious effort. "We can't carry it all."

The corpses they rolled into the pitfall, and covered them over. The net they hauled off into the underbrush. Then they sorted out the sequins, making three packs, two heavy and one light. There still remained a fortune in clears, milks, sards, deep blues and greens. These they wrapped into a fourth parcel, which they secreted under the roots of the great torquil.

Two hours remained until dusk. They took up their packs, went to the eastern edge of the forest, accommodating their gait to Traz. Here they argued the feasibility of camping until Traz's leg had healed. Traz would hear none of it. "I can keep up, so long as we don't have to run."

"Running won't help us in any case," said Reith.

"If they catch us," said Anacho, "then we must run. With nerve-fire at our necks."

The afternoon light deepened through gold and dark gold; Carina 4269 disappeared and sepia murk fell over the landscape. The hills showed minuscule flickers of flame. The three set forth, and so the dismal journey began: across the Stage from one black clump of dendron to another. At last they came to the slopes, and doggedly began to climb.

Dawn found them under the ridge, with both hunters and hunted already astir. Shelter was nowhere in sight; the three descended into a gulch and contrived a covert of dry brush.

The day advanced. Anacho and Reith dozed while Traz lay staring at the sky; the enforced idleness had caused his leg to stiffen. At noon a hunt of four proud Dirdir, resplendent in glittering casques, crossed the ravine. For a moment they paused, apparently sensing the near-presence of quarry, but other affairs attracted their attention and they continued off to the north.

The sun declined, illuminating the eastern wall of

the gulch. Anacho gave an uncharacteristic snort of laughter. "Look there." He pointed. Not twenty feet distant the ground had broken, revealing the wrinkled dome of a large mature node. "Scarlets at least. Maybe purples."

Reith made a gesture of sad resignation. "We can hardly carry the fortune we already have. It is sufficient."

"You underestimate the rapacity and greed of Sivishe," grumbled Anacho. "To do what you propose will require two fortunes, or more." He dug up the node. "A purple. We can't leave it behind."

"Very well," said Reith. "I'll carry it."

"No," said Traz. "I'll carry it. You two already have most of the load."

"We'll divide it into three parts," said Reith. "It won't be all that much more."

Night came at last; the three shouldered their packs and continued, Traz hopping, hobbling, grimacing in pain. Down the north slope they moved, and the closer they approached the Portal of Gleams, the more ghastly and detestable seemed the Zone.

Dawn found them at the base of the hills, with the Portal yet ten miles north. As they rested in a shadowed fissure, Reith swept the landscape through his scanscope. The Forelands seemed quiet and almost devoid of life. Far to the northwest a dozen shapes made for the Portal of Gleams, hoping to reach safety before full daylight. They ran with the peculiar scuttling gait that men instinctively used within the Zone, as if they thereby made themselves inconspicuous. A band of hunters stood on a relatively nearby crag, still and alert as eagles. They watched the fleeing men with regret. Reith put aside all hope of reaching the Portal before dark. The three passed another dreary day behind a boulder, with camouflage cloth overhead.

During the middle morning a sky-car drifted overhead. "They're looking for the missing hunts," said Anacho in a hushed voice. "Undoubtedly there will be a *tsau'gsh*. . . . We are in great danger."

Reith looked after the sky-car, then gauged the miles to the Portal. "By midnight we should be safe."

"We may not last till midnight, if the Dirdir close off the Forelands, as well they may do."

"We can't set out now; they'd take us for sure."

Anacho gave a dour nod. "Agreed."

Toward middle afternoon another sky-car came to hover over the Forelands. Anacho hissed between his teeth. "We are trapped." But after half an hour the sky-car once more drifted south beyond the hills.

Reith made a careful scrutiny of the landscape. "I see no hunts. Ten miles means at least two hours. Shall we make a run for it?"

Traz looked down at his leg with a wistful expression. "You two go on. I'll follow when the sun goes down."

"Too late by then," said Anacho. "Already it is too late."

Once more Reith searched the ridges. He helped Traz to his feet. "It's all of us or none."

They started out across the barrens, feeling naked and vulnerable. Any hunt which chanced to look down from the ridge into this particular sector could not fail to notice them.

They proceeded for half an hour, scuttling half-crouched like the others. From time to time Reith paused to sweep the landscape to the rear with his scanscope, dreading lest he see the dire shapes in pursuit. But the miles fell behind, and hope correspondingly began to rise. Traz's face was gray with pain and exhaustion; nevertheless he forced the pace, tottering at a half-run, until Reith suspected that he ran from sheer hysteria.

But suddenly Traz stopped. He looked back at the ridges. "They are watching us."

Reith scrutinized the ridges, slopes and dark gulches, but saw nothing. Traz had already set off at an erratic lope, with Anacho hunching along behind. Reith followed. A few hundred yards further north he paused again, and this time thought he saw a flicker of light reflecting from metal. Dirdir? Reith gauged the distance ahead. They had come roughly halfway across the barrens. Reith drew a deep breath and ran off after Traz and Anacho. Conceivably the Dirdir might not choose to pursue so far across the Forelands.

A second time he halted and looked back. All uncertainty was gone: four shapes bounded down the slopes. There could be no doubt as to their intent.

Reith caught up with Traz and Anacho. Traz ran with glaring eyes, mouth open so that his teeth showed. Reith took the heaviest bag from the lad's shoulder, threw it over his own. If anything, Traz slowed his pace a trifle. Anacho gauged the distance ahead, studied the pursuing Dirdir. "We have a chance."

The three ran, hearts pounding, lungs burning. Traz's face was like a skull. Anacho relieved him of the remaining parcel.

The Portal of Gleams was visible: a haven of wonderful security. Behind came the hunters, by prodigious leaps.

Traz was faltering, with the Portal yet a half-mile ahead. "Onmale!" called Reith.

The effect was startling. Traz seemed to expand, to grow tall. He stopped short and swung about to face the pursuers. His face was that of a stranger: a person sagacious, fierce and dominant—the personification in fact of the emblem of Onmale.

Onmale was too proud to flee.

"Run!" cried Reith in a panic. "If we must fight, let's fight on our own terms!"

Traz, or Onmale—the two were confused—seized a pack from Reith and one from Anacho and sprang ahead toward the Portal.

Reith wasted a half-second gauging the distance to the first Dirdir, then continued his flight. Traz soared across the barrens. Anacho, his face pink and distorted, pounded behind.

Traz gained the Portal. He turned and waited, catapult in one hand, sword in the other. Anacho passed through, then Reith, not fifty feet in advance of the

foremost Dirdir. Traz backed to stand just beyond the
boundary, challenging the Dirdir to attack. The Dirdir
gave a shrill scream of fury. It shook its head, and its
effulgences, standing high, vibrated. Then, curveting, it
loped south, after its comrades, already on their way
back to the hills.

Anacho leaned panting against the Portal of Gleams.
Reith stood with the breath rasping in his throat.
Traz's face was vacant and gray. His knees buckled; he
fell to the ground and lay quiet, giving not so much as
a twitch.

Reith staggered forward, turned him over. Traz
seemed not to breathe. Reith straddled his body and
applied artificial respiration. Traz gave a throat-
wrenching gasp. Presently he began to breathe evenly.

The solicitors, touts and beggars who normally kept
station by the Portal of Gleams had scattered, aghast at
the approach of the Dirdir. First to return was a young
man in a long maroon gown, who now stood making
gracious movements of concern. "An outrage," he la-
mented. "The conduct of the Dirdir! Never should they
chase so close to the gate! They have almost killed this
poor young man!"

"Quiet," snapped Anacho. "You disturb us."

The young man stood aside. Reith and Anacho lifted
Traz to his feet, where he stood in something of a stu-
por.

The young man once again came forward, his soft
brown eyes all-seeing, all-knowing. "Allow me to assist. I am Issam the Thang; I represent the Hopeful
Venture Inn, which promises a restful atmosphere. Allow me to assist with your parcels." Picking up Traz's
pack, he turned a startled gaze toward Reith and Anacho. "Sequins?"

Anacho seized the pack. "Be off with you! Our plans
are established!"

"As you will," said Issam the Thang, "but the Hopeful Venture Inn is near at hand, and something apart
from the tumult and gaming. While comfortable, the

expense does not approach the exorbitant fees of the Alawan."

"Very well," said Reith. "Take us to the Hopeful Venture."

Anacho muttered under his breath; to which Issam the Thang made a delicate gesture of reproach. "This way, if you will."

They trudged toward Maust, Traz hobbling on his lame leg.

"My memory is a jumble," he muttered. "I recall crossing the Forelands; I remember that someone shouted into my ear—"

"It was I," said Reith.

"—then after, nothing real, and next I lay beside the Portal." And a moment later he mused: "I heard roaring voices. A thousand faces looked past me, warriors' faces, raging. I have seen such things in dreams." His voice dwindled; he said no more.

Chapter 7

The Hopeful Venture Inn stood at the back of a narrow alley, a brooding, age-blackened structure, doing no great business, to judge from the common room, which was dark and still. Issam, it now appeared, was the proprietor. He made an effusive show of hospitality, ordering water, lamps and linen up to the "grand suite," which orders were effected by a surly servant with enormous red hands and a shock of coarse red hair. The three mounted a twisting stairway to the suite, which comprised a sitting-room, a wash-room, several irregular alcoves furnished with sour-smelling couches. The servant arranged the lamps, brought flasks of wine and departed. Anacho examined the lead and wax stoppers, then put the flasks aside. "Too much risk of drugs or poison. When the man awakes—if he awakes—his sequins are gone and he is bereft. I am dissatisfied; we would have done better at the Alawan."

"Tomorrow is time enough," said Reith, sinking into a chair with a groan of fatigue.

"Tomorrow we must be gone from Maust," said Anacho. "If we are not marked men now, we soon will be." He went forth and presently returned with bread, meat and wine.

They ate and drank; then Anacho checked the bars and bolts. "Who knows what transpires in these old piles? A knife in the dark, a single sound, and who is the wiser save Issam the Thang?"

Again checking the locks, the three prepared themselves for sleep, Anacho, declaring himself to be easily aroused, put the sequins between himself and the wall. Except for a single wavering night light the lamps were extinguished. A few moments later Anacho slipped noiselessly across the room to Reith's couch. "I suspect peepholes and listening pipes," he whispered. "Here—the sequins. Put them beside you. Let us sit quietly and watch for a period."

Reith forced himself into a state of alertness. Fatigue defeated him; his eyelids drooped. He slept.

Time passed. Reith was aroused by a prod from Anacho's elbow; he sat up with a jerk of guilt. "Quiet," said Anacho in the ghost of a whisper. "Look yonder."

Reith peered through the darkness. A scrape, a movement in the shadows, a dark shape—a light suddenly flared up. Traz stood, crouched and glaring, arms concealed in the shadow of his body.

The two men by Anacho's couch turned to face the lamp, faces blank and startled. One was Issam the Thang; the second was the burly servant who had been groping with his enormous hands for the neck of Anacho, presumably asleep on the couch. The servant emitted a curious whisper of excitement and hopped across the room, hands clutching. Traz fired his catapult into the twisted face. The man fell silently, going to oblivion without apprehension or regret. Issam sprang for an opening in the wall. Reith bore him to the floor. Issam fought desperately; for all his slenderness and delicacy he was as strong and quick as a serpent. Reith seized him in an arm-lock and jerked him erect, squeaking in pain.

Anacho flipped a cord around Issam's neck and prepared to tighten the noose. Reith grimaced but made no protest. This was the justice of Maust; it was only fitting that here, in the flaring lamplight, Issam should go to his doom.

Issam fervently cried out: "No! I am only a miserable Thang! Don't kill me! I'll help you, I swear! I'll help you escape!"

"Wait," said Reith. To Issam: "How do you mean, help us escape? Are we in danger?"

"Yes, of course. What should you expect?"

"Tell me of this danger."

Sensing reprieve, Issam drew himself up, indignantly shrugged away Anacho's hands. "The information is valuable. How much will you pay?"

Reith nodded to Anacho. "Proceed."

Issam gave a heart-rending wail. "No, no! Trade me my life for your three lives—is that not enough?"

"If such be the case."

"It is the case. Stand back, then; remove the noose."

"Not until we know the kind of bargain we are making."

Issam looked from face to face and saw nothing to encourage him. "Well, then, secret word has come to me. The Dirdir are in a state of frothing fury. Someone has destroyed an unlikely number of hunting parties, and stolen the booty—as much as two hundred thousands' worth of sequins. Special agents are on watch—here and elsewhere. Whoever submits any information will derive great benefit. If you are the persons of the case, as I suspect, you will never leave Maust except in prickle-collars—unless I help you."

Reith asked cautiously, "Help us how?"

"I can and will save you—for a price."

Reith looked toward Anacho, who drew taut the

cord. Issam clawed at the constriction, eyes bulging in the lamplight. The noose loosened. Issam croaked, "My life for yours, that is our bargain."

"Then talk no more of 'price.' Needless to say, don't try to trick us."

"Never, never!" croaked Issam. "I live or die with you! Your life is my life! We must leave now. Morning will be too late."

"Leave how? Afoot?"

"It may not be necessary. Make yourselves ready. Do those bags and parcels actually contain sequins?"

"Scarlets and purples," said Anacho with sadistic relish. "If you want the same, go into the Zone and kill Dirdir."

Issam shuddered. "Are you ready?" He waited impatiently while the three resumed their garments. On sudden thought he dropped down to rifle the corpse of the servant and clucked with satisfaction at the handful of clears and milks he found in the pouch.

The three were ready. In spite of Issam's protest Anacho maintained the noose around his neck. "So that you will not misunderstand our intentions."

"Must I always be cursed with suspicious associates?"

The main avenue of Maust vibrated with movement, the shift of faces, colored lights; from the taverns came wailing music, drunken belches of laughter, an occasional angry outcry. By furtive shortcuts and dark detours Issam took them to a stable at the north of town, where a scowling attendant finally responded to Issam's pounding. Five minutes of surly haggling resulted in the saddling of four leap-horses; ten minutes later, as the moons Az and Braz simultaneously rolled up the eastern sky, Reith, Anacho, Traz and Issam bounded north on the gaunt white leap-horses of Kachan, and left Maust behind.

Through the night they rode and at dawn entered Khorai. Smoke trickling up from iron chimneys drifted north over the First Sea, which by some trick of light appeared as black as a sea of pitch, with the plum-colored northern sky for a backdrop.

Through Khorai they pounded and down to the harbor where they dismounted. Issam, wearing the most modest of smiles, bowed to Reith, hands folded behind his dark red gown. "I have achieved my goal; my friends have been delivered safe to Khorai."

"The friends you hoped to strangle a few hours ago."

Issam's smile became tremulous. "That was Maust! One's behavior in Maust must be tolerated."

"As far as I am concerned, you may return."

Issam bowed low once more. "May nine-headed Sagorio maim your enemies! So now, farewell!" Issam took the pale leap-horses back through Khorai and disappeared to the south.

The sky-car rested where they had left it. As they climbed aboard, the harbor master looked on with a saturnine sneer, but made no comment. Mindful of Khor truculence the three took pains to ignore his presence.

The sky-car rose into the morning sky, curved along the shore of the First Sea. So began the first stage of the journey to Sivishe.

Chapter 8

The sky-car flew west. To the south spread a vast dusty desert; to the north lay the First Sea. Below and ahead mud-flats alternated with promontories of sandstone in a monotonous succession, one beyond the other, into the haze at the limit of vision.

Traz slept the sleep of sheer exhaustion. Anacho, to the contrary, sat unconcerned and careless, as if fear and emergency were foreign to his experience. Reith, though he ached with fatigue, could not wrench his gaze away from the radar screen, except to search the sky. Anacho's carefree manner at last became exasperating. Reith glared at him through red-rimmed eyes and spoke in a dour voice: "For a fugitive you show surprisingly little apprehension. I admire your composure."

Anacho made an easy gesture. "What you call composure is child-like faith. I have become superstitious. Consider: we have entered the Carabas, killed dozens of First Folk and carried off their sequins. So now, how can I take seriously the prospect of casual interception?"

"Your faith is greater than mine," growled Reith. "I expect the whole force of the Dirdir system to be scouring the skies for us."

Anacho gave an indulgent laugh. "That is not the Dirdir way! You project your own concepts into the Dirdir mind. Remember, they do not look upon organization as an end in itself; this is a human attribute. The Dirdir exists only as himself, a creature responsible only to his pride. He cooperates with his fellows when the prospects suit him."

Reith shook his head skeptically, and went back to studying the radar-screen. "There must be more to it than that. How does the society hold together? How can the Dirdir sustain long-term projects?"

"Very simple. One Dirdir is much like another; there are racial forces which compel all alike. In great dilution, the submen know these forces as 'tradition,' 'caste authority,' 'zest to over-achieve'; in the Dirdir society they become compulsions. The individual is bound to customs of the race. Should a Dirdir need assistance he need only cry out *hs'ai hs'ai, hs'ai,* and he is helped. If a Dirdir is wronged, he calls *dr'ssa, dr'ssa, dr'ssa* and commands arbitration. If the arbitration fails to suit him he can challenge the arbitrator, who is usually an Excellence; if he defeats the arbitrator, he is vindicated. More often he himself is defeated; his efful-

gences are plucked out and he becomes a pariah. . . .
There are few challenges of arbitration."

"Under such conditions, the society would seem to
be highly conservative."

"This is the case, until there is need for change, and
then the Dirdir applies himself to the problem with
'zest to over-achieve.' He is capable of creative thinking; his brain is supple and responsive; he wastes no
energy upon mannerism. Multiple sexuality and the
'secrets' of course are a distraction, but like the hunt
they are a source of violent passion beyond human
comprehension."

"All this to the side, why should they give up the
search for us so easily?"

"Is it not clear?" demanded Anacho testily. "How
could even the Dirdir suspect that we fly toward
Sivishe in a sky-car? Nothing identifies the men sought
at Smargash with the men who destroyed Dirdir in the
Carabas. Perhaps in time a connection will be made, if,
for example, Issam the Thang is questioned. Until then
they are ignorant that we fly a sky-car. So why put up
search-screens?"

"I hope you're right," said Reith.

"We shall see. Meanwhile—we are alive. We fly a
sky-car in comfort. We carry better than two hundred
thousand sequins. Notice ahead: Cape Braize! Beyond
lies the Schanizade. We will now alter course and come
down upon Haulk from above. Who will notice a single
sky-car among a hundred? At Sivishe we will mingle
with the multitude, while the Dirdir seek us across the
Zhaarken, or at Jalkh, or out on the Hunghus tundra."

Ten miles passed below the sky-car, with Reith pon-
dering the soul of the Dirdir race. He asked, "Suppose
you or I were in trouble and cried *dr'ssa dr'ssa,
dr'ssa?*"

"That is the call for arbitration. *Hs'ai hs'ai, hs'ai* is
the cry for help."

"Very well, *hs'ai hs'ai, h'sai*—would a Dirdir be im-
pelled to help?"

"Yes, by the force of tradition. This is automatic, a

reflexive act: the connective tissue which binds an otherwise wild and mercurial race."

Two hours before sunset a storm blew in from the Schanizade. Carina 4269 became a brown wraith, then disappeared as black clouds tumbled up the sky. Surf like dirty beer-foam swept across the beach, close to the boles of the black dendrons which shrouded the foreshore. The upper fronds twisted to gusts of wind, turning up glossy gray undersides; roiling patterns moved across the black upper surfaces.

The sky-car fled south through the umber dusk, then, with the last glimmer of light, landed in the lee of a basalt jut. The three, huddling upon the settees and ignoring the odor of Dirdir bodies, slept while the storm hissed through the rocks.

Dawn brought a strange illumination, like light shining through brown bottle-glass. There was neither food nor drink in the sky-car, but pilgrim pod grew out on the barrens and a brackish river flowed nearby. Traz went quietly along the bank, craning his neck to peer through the reflections. He stopped short, crouched, plunged into the water to emerge with a yellow creature, all thrashing tentacles and jointed legs, which he and Anacho devoured raw. Reith stolidly ate pilgrim pod.

With the meal finished they leaned back against the sky-car, basking in the honey-colored sunlight and enjoying the morning calm. "Tomorrow," said Anacho, "we arrive in Sivishe. Our life once more changes. We are no longer thieves and desperadoes, but men of substance, or so we must let it appear."

"Very well," said Reith. "What next?"

"We must be subtle. We do not simply apply at the spaceyards with our money."

"Hardly," said Reith. "On Tschai whatever seems reasonable is wrong."

"It is impossible," said Anacho, "to function without the support of an influential person. This will be our first concern."

"A Dirdir? Or a Dirdirman?"

"Sivishe is a city of submen; the Dirdir and Dirdirmen keep to Hei on the mainland. You will see."

Chapter 9

Haulk hung like a cramped and distorted appendix from the distended belly of Kislovan, with the Schanizade Ocean to the west and the Gulf of Ajzan to the east. At the head of the gulf was the island Sivishe, with an untidy industrial jumble at the northern end. A causeway led to the mainland and Hei, the Dirdir city. At the center of Hei and dominating the entire landscape stood a box of gray glass five miles long, three miles wide, a thousand feet high: a structure so large that the perspectives seemed distorted. A forest of spires surrounded the box, a tenth as high, scarlet and purple, then mauve, gray and white toward the periphery.

Anacho indicated the towers. "Each houses a clan. Someday I will describe the life of Hei: the promenades, the secrets of multiple sex, the castes and clans. But of more immediate interest, yonder lie the spaceyards."

Reith saw an area at the center of the island surrounded by shops, warehouses, depots and hangars. Six large spaceships and three smaller craft occupied bays to one side. Anacho's voice broke into his speculations.

"The spaceships are well secured. The Dirdir are far more stringent than the Wankh—by instinct rather than by reason, for no one in history has stolen a spaceship."

"No one in history has come with two hundred thousand sequins. Such money will grease a lot of palms."

"What good are sequins in the Glass Box?"

Reith said no more. Anacho took the sky-car down to a paved area beside the spaceyards.

"Now," said Anacho in a calm voice, "we shall learn our destiny."

Reith took instant alarm. "What do you mean by that?"

"If we have been traced, if we are expected, then we will be taken; and soon there will be an end to us. But the car yard seems as usual; I expect no disaster. Remember now, this is Sivishe. I am the Dirdirman, you are the submen; act accordingly."

Reith dubiously searched the yard. As Anacho had stated there seemed no untoward activity.

The sky-car landed. The three alighted. Anacho stood austerely aside while Reith and Traz removed the packs.

A power-wagon approached and fixed clamps to the sky-car. The operator, a hybrid of Dirdirman and another race unknown, inspected Anacho with impersonal curiosity, ignoring Reith and Traz. "What is to be the disposition?"

"Temporary deposit, on call," said Anacho.

"To what charge?"

"Special. I'll take the token."

"Number sixty-four." The clerk gave Anacho a brass disk. "I require twenty sequins."

"Twenty, and five for yourself."

The lift-wagon conveyed the sky-car to a numbered slot. Anacho led the way to a slide-way, with Reith and Traz trudging behind with the packs. They stepped aboard and were conveyed out to a wide avenue, along which ran a considerable traffic of power-wagons, passenger cars, drays.

Here Anacho paused to reflect. "I have been gone so long, I have traveled so far, that Sivishe is somewhat strange. First, of course, we need lodgings. Across the avenue, as I recall, is a suitable inn."

At the Ancient Realm Inn the three were led down a white- and black-tiled corridor to a suite overlooking the central court, where a dozen women sat on benches watching the windows for a signal.

Two seemed to be Dirdirwomen: thin sharp-faced creatures, pallid as snow, with a sparse fuzz of gray hair at the back of their scalps. Anacho surveyed them thoughtfully for a moment or so, then turned away. "We are fugitives, of course," he said, "and we must be wary. Nevertheless, here in Sivishe where many people come and go, we are as safe as we might be anywhere. The Dirdir do not concern themselves with Sivishe unless circumstances fail to suit them, in which case the Administrator goes to the Glass Box. Otherwise, the Administrator has a free hand; he taxes, polices, judges, punishes, appropriates as he sees fit and is therefore the least corruptible man in Sivishe. For influential assistance we must seek elsewhere; tomorrow I will make inquiry. Next we will need a structure of suitable dimensions, close by the spaceyards, yet inconspicuous. Again, a matter requiring discreet inquiry. Then—most sensitive of all—we must hire technical personnel to assemble the components and perform the necessary tuning and phasing. If we pay high wages we can no doubt secure the right men. I will represent myself as a Dirdirman Superior—in fact, my former status—and hint of Dirdir reprisals against loose-mouthed men. There is no reason why the project should not go easily and smoothly, except for the innate perversity of circumstances."

"In other words," said Reith, "the chances are against us."

Anacho ignored the remark. "A warning: the city seethes with intrigue. Folk come to Sivishe for a single purpose: to win advantage. The city is a turmoil of illicit activity, robbery, extortion, vice, gambling, gluttony, extravagant display, swindling. These are endemic, and the victim has small hope of recourse. The Dirdir are unconcerned; the antics and maneuvers of the submen are nothing to them. The Administrator is interested only in maintaining order. So: caution!

Trust no one; answer no questions! Identify yourselves
as steppe-men seeking employment; profess stupidity.
By such means we minimize risk."

Chapter 10

In the morning Anacho went forth to make his inquiries. Reith and Traz descended to the street café
and sat watching the passersby. Traz was displeased
with everything he saw. "All cities are vile," he
grumbled. "This is the worst: a detestable place. Do
you notice the stink? Chemicals, smoke, disease, rotting
stone. The smell has infected the folk; observe their
faces."

Reith could not deny that the inhabitants of Sivishe
were an unprepossessing lot. Their complexions ranged
from muddy brown to Dirdirman white; their physiog-
nomies reflected thousands of years of half-purposeful
mutation. Never had Reith seen so wary and self-con-
tained a people. Living in contiguity with an alien
race had fostered no fellowship: in Sivishe each man
was a stranger. As a positive consequence, Reith and
Traz were inconspicuous: no one looked twice in their
direction.

Reith sat musing over his bowl of pale wine, relaxed
and almost at peace. As he pondered old Tschai, it occurred to him the single homogenizing force was the
language, the same across the entire planet. Perhaps
because communication often represented the differ-
ence between life and death, because those who failed
to communicate died, the language had retained its uni-
versality. Presumably the language had its roots on ancient Earth. It resembled no language with which he
was familiar. He considered key words. *Vam* was
'mother'; *tatap* was 'father'; *issir* was 'sword.' The

cardinal numbers were *aine, sei, dros, enser, nif, hisz, yaga, managa, nuwai, tix*. No significant parallels, but somehow, a haunting echo of Earth sounds. . . .

In general, reflected Reith, life on Tschai ranged a wider gamut than did life on Earth. Passions were more intense: grief more poignant, joy more exalted. Personalities were more decisive. By contrast the folk of Earth seemed pensive, conditional, sedate. Laughter on Earth was less boisterous; still, there were fewer gasps of horror.

As he often did, Reith wondered: *Suppose I return to Earth, what then? Can I adjust to an existence so placid and staid? Or all my life will I long for the steppes and seas of Tschai?* Reith gave a sad chuckle. A problem he would be glad to confront.

Anacho returned. After a quick glance to left and right he settled himself at the table. His manner was subdued. "I've been optimistic," he muttered. "I've trusted too much to my memories."

"How so?" Reith demanded.

"Nothing immediate. It seems, merely, that I have underestimated our impact on the times. Twice this morning I heard talk of the madmen who invaded the Carabas and slaughtered Dirdir as if they were lippets. Hei throbs with agitation and anger, or so it is said. Various *tsau'gsh* are in progress; all would regret to be the madmen once they are captured."

Traz was outraged. "The Dirdir go to the Carabas to kill men," he stormed. "Why should they resent the case when they themselves are killed?"

"Hist!" exclaimed Anacho. "Not so loud! Do you wish to attract attention? In Sivishe no one blurts forth his thoughts; it is unwholesome!"

"Another black mark against this squalid city!" declared Traz, but in a more restrained voice.

"Come now," said Anacho nervously. "It is not so disheartening after all. Think of it! While Dirdir range the continents, we three rest in Sivishe, at the Ancient Realm Inn."

"A precarious satisfaction," said Reith. "What else did you learn?"

"The Administrator is Clodo Erlius. He has just assumed office—not necessarily advantageous from our point of view since a new official is apt to stringency. I have made guarded inquiries, and since I am a Dirdirman Superior, I did not encounter total frankness. However a certain name has been mentioned twice. That name is Aila Woudiver. His ostensible occupation is the supply and transport of structural materials. He is a notable gourmand and voluptuary, with tastes at once so refined, so gross and so inordinate as to cost him vast sums. This information was given freely, in a tone of envious admiration. Woudiver's illicit capabilities were merely implied."

"Woudiver would appear to be an unsavory colleague," said Reith.

Anacho snorted in derision. "You demand that I find someone proficient at conniving, chicanery, theft; when I produce this man, you look down your nose at him."

Reith grinned. "No other names were mentioned?"

"Another source explained, in a carefully facetious manner, that any extraordinary activity must surely attract the attention of Woudiver. It would seem that he is the man with whom we must deal. In a certain sense, his reputation is reassuring; he is necessarily competent."

Traz entered the conversation. "What if this Woudiver refuses to help us? Are we not then at his mercy? Could he not extort our sequins from us?"

Anacho pursed his lips, shrugged. "No scheme of this sort is absolutely reliable. Aila Woudiver would seem to be a sound choice, from our point of view. He has access to the sources of supply, he controls transport vehicles, and possibly he can provide a suitable building in which to assemble a space-boat."

Reith said reluctantly, "We want the most competent man, and if we get him I suppose we can't cavil at his personal attributes. Still, on the other hand . . . Oh, well. What pretext should we use?"

"The tale you gave the Lokhars—that we need a spaceship to take possession of a treasure—is as good as any. Woudiver will discredit all he is told; he will expect duplicity, so one tale is as good as another."

Traz muttered: "Attention! Dirdir are approaching."

There were three, striding with a protentous gait. Cages of silver mesh clung to the back of their bone-white heads; the effulgences splayed down to either side of their shoulders. Flaps of soft pale leather hung from their arms, almost to the ground. Other strips hung down front and back, indited with vertical rows of red and black circular symbols.

"Inspectors," muttered Anacho through down-drooping lips. "Not once a year do they come to Sivishe—unless complaints are made."

"Will they know you for a Dirdirman?"

"Of course. I hope they do not know me for Ankhe at afram Anacho, the fugitive."

The Dirdir passed; Reith glanced at them indifferently, though his flesh crept at their proximity. They ignored the three and continued along the avenue, pale leather flaps swinging to their stride.

Anacho's face relaxed from its glare of tension. In a subdued voice, Reith said, "The sooner we leave Sivishe the better."

Anacho drummed his fingers on the table and gave a final decisive rap. "Very well. I will telephone Aila Woudiver and arrange an exploratory meeting." He stepped into the inn and presently returned. "A car will arrive shortly to pick us up."

Reith had not been ready for so swift a response. "What did you tell him?" he asked uneasily.

"That we wanted to consult him in regard to a business matter."

"Hmf." Reith leaned back in his chair. "Too much haste is as bad as too little."

Anacho threw up his hands in vexation and defeat. "What reason to delay?"

"No real one. I feel strange to Sivishe and unsure of my responses——hence worried."

"No worry there. With familiarity Sivishe becomes even less reassuring."

Reith said no more. Fifteen minutes later an antique black vehicle, which at one time had been a grand saloon, halted in front of the hotel. A middle-aged man, harsh and grim, looked forth. He jerked his head toward Anacho. "You await a car?"

"To Woudiver?"

"Get in."

The three climbed into the vehicle, seated themselves on benches. The car rolled at no great speed down the avenue, then, turning off toward the south, entered a district of slatternly apartment houses: buildings erected with neither judgment or precision. No two doorways were alike; windows of irregular shape and size opened at random in the thick walls. Wan-faced folk stood in alcoves or peered down into the streets; all turned to watch the passage of the car. "Laborers," said Anacho with a sniff of distaste. "Kherman, Thangs, Sad Islanders. They come from all Kislovan and lands beyond, as well."

The car continued across a littered plaza, into a street of small shops, all fitted with heavy metal shutters. Anacho asked the driver, "How far to Woudiver's?"

"Not far." The reply was uttered with hardly a motion of the lips.

"Where does he live? Out on the Heights?"

"On Zamia Rise."

Reith considered the hooked nose, the dour cords of muscle around the colorless mouth: the face of an executioner.

The way led up a low hill. The houses became abandoned gardens. The car halted at the end of a lane. The driver with a curt gesture signaled the three to alight, then silently led them along a shadowy passage smelling of dankness and mold, through an archway, across a courtyard, up a shallow flight of stairs into a room with walls of mustard-colored tile.

"Wait here." He passed through a door of black psilla bound with iron, and a moment later looked forth. He crooked his finger. "Come."

The three filed into a large white-walled chamber. A scarlet and maroon rug muffled the floor; for furniture there were settees padded with pink, red and yellow plush, a heavy table of carved wax-wood, a censer exuding wisps of heavy smoke. Behind the table stood an enormous yellow-skinned man in robes of red, black and ivory. His face was round as a melon; a few strands of sandy hair lay across his mottled pate. He was a man vast in every dimension, and motivated, so it seemed to Reith, by a grandiose and cynical intelligence. He spoke. "I am Aila Woudiver." His voice was under exquisite control; now it was soft and fluting. "I see a Dirdirman of the First—"

"Superior!" Anacho corrected.

"—a youth of a rough unknown race, a man of even more doubtful extraction. Why does such an ill-matched trio seek me out?"

"To discuss a matter possibly of mutual interest," said Reith.

The lower third of Woudiver's face trembled in a grin. "Continue."

Reith looked around the room, then turned back to Woudiver. "I suggest that we move to another location, out of doors, by preference."

Woudiver's thin, almost-nonexistent eyebrows lofted high in surprise. "I fail to understand. Will you explain?"

"Certainly, if we can move to another area."

Woudiver frowned in sudden petulance, but marched forward. The three followed him through an archway, up a ramp and out on a deck which overlooked a vast hazy distance to the west. Woudiver spoke in a voice now carefully resonant: "Does this situation seem suitable?"

"Better," said Reith.

"You puzzle me," said Woudiver, settling into a massive chair. "What noxious influence do you so dread?"

Reith looked meaningfully across the panorama, toward the colored towers and cloud-gray Glass Box of far Hei. "You are an important man. Your activities conceivably interest certain folk to the extent that they monitor your conversations."

Woudiver made a jovial gesture. "Your business appears highly confidential, or even illicit."

"Does this alarm you?"

Woudiver pursed his lips into a fountain of gray-pink gristle. "Let us get down to affairs."

"Certainly. Are you interested in gaining wealth?"

"Poof," said Woudiver. "I have enough for my small needs. But anyone can use more money."

"In essence, the situation is this: we know where and how to obtain a considerable treasure, at no risk."

"You are the most fortunate of men!"

"Certain preparations are necessary. We believe that you, a man of known resource, will be able to provide assistance in return for a share of the gain. I do not, of course, refer to financial assistance."

"I cannot say yes or no until I am apprised of all details," said Woudiver in the most suave of voices. "Naturally, you may speak without reserve; my reputation for discretion is a byword."

"First we need a clear indication of your interest. Why waste time for nothing?"

Woudiver blinked. "I am as interested as is possible in a factual vacuum."

"Very well, then. Our problem is this: we must procure a small spaceship."

Woudiver sat motionless, his eyes boring into Reith's face. He glanced swiftly at Traz and Anacho, then gave a short brisk laugh. "You credit me with remarkable powers! Not to say reckless audacity! How can I possibly provide a spaceship, large or small? Either you are madmen or you take me for one!"

Reith smiled at Woudiver's vehemence, which he diagnosed as a tactical device. "We have considered the situation carefully," said Reith. "The project is not impossible with the help of a person such as yourself."

Woudiver gave his great lemon-colored head a peevish shake. "So I merely point my finger toward the Grand Spaceyards and produce a ship? Is this your belief? You would have me bounding through the Glass Cage before the day was out."

"Remember," said Reith, "a large vessel is not necessary. Conceivably we could acquire an obsolete craft and put it into workable condition. Or we might obtain components from persons who could be induced to sell, and assemble them in a makeshift hull."

Woudiver sat pulling at his chin. "The Dirdir certainly would oppose such a project."

"I mentioned the need for discretion," said Reith.

Woudiver puffed out his cheeks. "How much wealth is involved? What is the nature of this wealth? Where is it located?"

"These are details which at the moment can have no real interest for you," said Reith.

Woudiver tapped his chin with a yellow forefinger. "Let us discuss the matter as an asbtraction. First, the practicalities. A large sum of money would be required: for inducements, technical help, a suitable place of assembly, and of course for the components you mention. Where would this money come from?" His voice took on a sardonic resonance. "You did not expect financing from Aila Woudiver?"

"Financing is no problem," said Reith. "We have ample funds."

"Indeed!" Woudiver was impressed. "How much, may I ask, are you prepared to spend?"

"Oh, fifty to a hundred thousand sequins."

Woudiver gave his head a shake of indulgent amusement. "A hundred thousand would be barely adequate." He turned a glance toward Hei. "I could never concern myself in any illicit or forbidden enterprise."

"Naturally not."

"I might be able to advise you, on a friendly and informal basis, for, say, a fixed fee, or perhaps a percentage of outlay, and a small share in any eventual rewards."

"Something of the sort might suit our needs," said Reith. "How long, at an estimate, would such a project require?"

"Who knows? Who can prophesy such things? A month? Two months? Information is essential, which we now lack. A knowledgeable person from the Grand Spaceyards must be consulted."

"Knowledgeable, competent, and trustworthy," amended Reith.

"That goes without saying. I know the very man, a person for whom I have done several favors. In the course of a day or two I will see him and bring up the matter."

"Why not now?" asked Reith. "The sooner the better."

Woudiver raised a hand. "Haste leads to miscalculation. Come back in two days; I may have news for you. But first the matter of finance. I cannot invest my time without a retainer. I will need a small sum—say five thousand sequins—as earnest-money."

Reith shook his head. "I'll show you five thousand." He produced a card of purple sequins. "In fact here is twenty thousand. But we can't afford to spend a sequin except on actual costs."

Woudiver's face was one vast hurt. "What of my fee, then? Must I toil for joy alone?"

"Of course not. If all goes well, you will be rewarded to your satisfaction."

"This must serve for the moment," declared Woudiver in sudden heartiness. "In two days I will send Artilo for you. Discuss the matter with no one! Secrecy is absolutely essential!"

"This we well understand. In two days then."

Chapter 11

Sivishe was a dull city, gray and subdued, as if oppressed by the proximity of Hei. The great homes of Prospect Heights and Zamia Rise were pretentious enough, but lacked style and finesse. The folk of Sivishe were no less dull: a somber, humorless race, gray-skinned and tending toward overweight. At their meals they consumed great bowls of clabber, platters of boiled tuber, meat and fish seasoned with a rancid black sauce that numbed Reith's palate, though Anacho declared that the sauce occurred in numerous variants and was in fact a cultivated taste. For organized entertainment there were daily races, run not by animals but by men. On the day after the meeting with Woudiver, the three watched one of the races. Eight men participated, wearing garments of different colors and carrying a pole topped with a fragile glass globe. The runners not only sought to outrun their opponents but also to trip them by agile side-kicks, so that they fell and broke their glass globes, and were hence disqualified. The spectators numbered twenty thousand and maintained a low guttural howl during the duration of each race. Reith noticed a number of Dirdirmen among the spectators. They bet with as much verve as anyone, but kept themselves fastidiously apart. Reith wondered that Anacho would risk recognition by some previous acquaintance, to which Anacho gave a bitter laugh.

"Wearing these clothes I am safe. They will never see me. If I wore Dirdirman clothes I would be recognized at once and reported to the Castigators. Already I have seen half a dozen former acquaintances. None have so much as glanced at me."

The three visited the Grand Sivishe Spaceyards, where they strolled around the periphery observing the activity within. The spaceships were long, spindle-shaped, with intricate fins and sponsons—totally different from the bulky Wankh vessels and the flamboyant craft of the Blue Chasche, just as these differed from the starships of Earth.

The yards appeared to operate at less than top efficiency and far below capacity; even so, a respectable volume of work was in progress. Two cargo vessels were in the process of overhaul; a passenger ship seemed to be under construction. Elsewhere they noted three smaller ships, apparently uncommissioned warcraft, five or six space-boats in various stages of repair, a clutter of hulks on a junk heap to the rear of the shop. At the opposite end of the spaceyard three ships in commission rested on large black circles.

"They fare occasionally to Sibol," said Anacho. "There is no great traffic. Long ago when the Expansionists held sway Dirdir ships went out to many worlds. No longer. The Dirdir are quiescent. They would like to force the Wankh off of Tschai and slaughter the Blue Chasche, but they do not marshal their energies. It is somehow frightening. They are a terrible and active race and cannot lie quiet too long. One of these days they must explode, and go forth again."

"What of the Pnume?" Reith asked.

"There is no established pattern." Anacho pointed to the palisades behind Hei. "Through your electric telescope you might see Pnume warehouses, where they store metals for trade with the Dirdir. Pnumekin occasionally come out into Sivishe for one purpose or another. There are tunnels through all the hills and out into the country beyond. The Pnume observe every move the Dirdir make. They never come forth, however, for fear of the Dirdir, who kill them for vermin. On the other hand a Dirdir who goes hunting alone may never return. The Pnume have taken him down into their tunnels, so it is believed."

"It could only happen on Tschai," said Reith. "The folk trade in mutual detestation and kill each other on sight."

Anacho gave a sour snort. "I see nothing remarkable in the fact. The trading conduces to mutual profit; the killing gratifies the mutual detestation. The institutions have no common ground."

"What of the Pnumekin? Do the Dirdir or Dirdirmen molest them?"

"Not in Sivishe. A truce is observed. Elsewhere they too are destroyed, though rarely do they show themselves. There are, after all, relatively few Pnumekin, who must be the strangest and most remarkable folk of Tschai. . . . We must depart before we attract the attention of the yard police."

"Too late," said Traz in a dreary voice. "We are being watched at this moment."

"By whom?"

"Behind us, along the way, stand two men. One wears a brown jacket and a loose black hat; the other a dark blue cloak and the head-shroud."

Anacho glanced along the avenue. "They are not police—at least not yard guards."

The three turned back to the dingy jumble of concrete which marked the center of Sivishe. Carina 4269, glowing through a high layer of haze, cast cool brown light over the landscape. Full in the light came the two men, and something in their noiseless gait sent a pang of panic through Reith. "Who can they be?" he muttered.

"I don't know." Anacho turned a quick glance over his shoulder, but the men were no more than silhouettes against the light. "I don't think they are Dirdirmen. We have been in contact with Aila Woudiver; it may be that he is watched. Woudiver's own men conceivably. Or a criminal gang? After all, we might have been noticed coming down in the sky-car, or taking sequins to the vaults— Worse! Our descriptions from Maust may have been circulated. We are not undistinctive."

Reith said grimly, "We'll have to find out, one way

or another. Notice where the street passes close to that
broken building."

"Suitable."

The three strolled past a crumbling buttress of concrete, then, once out of sight, jumped to the side and
waited. The two men came running past on long noiseless strides. As they passed the buttress, Reith tackled
one, Anacho and Traz seized the other. With a sudden
exclamation Anacho and Traz released their grip. For
an instant Reith sensed a curious rancid odor, like
camphor and sour milk. Then a bone-racking shudder
of electricity sent him lurching back. He gave a croak
of dismay. The two men fled.

"I saw them," said Anacho in a subdued voice.
"They were Pnumekin, or perhaps Gzhindra. Did they
wear boots? Pnumekin walk with bare feet."

Reith went to look after the pair, but in some mirac-
ulous fashion they had disappeared. "What are Gzhindra?"

"Pnumekin outcasts."

The three trudged back through the dank streets of
Sivishe.

Anacho presently said, "It might have been worse."

"But why should Pnumekin follow us?"

Traz muttered, "They have been following us since
we departed Settra. And maybe before."

"The Pnume think strange thoughts," said Anacho
in a heavy voice. "Their actions seldom admit of sensible explanation; they are the stuff of Tschai itself."

Chapter 12

The three sat at a table outside the Ancient Realm
Inn, sipping soft wine and watching the passing folk of
Sivishe. Music was the key to a people's genius,

thought Reith. This morning, passing a tavern, he had
listened to the music of Sivishe. The orchestra consist-
ed of four instruments. The first was a bronze box
studded with vellum-wrapped cones which when
rubbed produced a sound like a cornet played at the
lowest possible range. The second, a vertical wooden
tube a foot in diameter, with twelve strings across
twelve slots, emitted resonant twanging arpeggios. The
third, a battery of forty-two drums, contributed a complex muffled rhythm. The fourth, a wooden slide-horn,
bleated, honked and produced wonderful squealing
glissandos as well.

The music performed by the ensemble seemed to
Reith peculiarly simple and limited: a repetition of
simple melody, played with only the smallest variation.
A few folk danced: men and women, face to face,
hands at sides, hopping carefully from one leg to the
other. Dull! thought Reith. Yet, at the end of the tune
the couples separated with expressions of triumph, and
recommenced their exertions as soon as the music
started again. As minutes passed, Reith began to sense
complexities, almost imperceptible variations. Like the
rancid black sauce which drowned the food, the music
required an intensive effort even to ingest; appreciation
and pleasure must remain forever beyond the reach of
a stranger. Perhaps, thought Reith, these almost-
unheard quavers and hesitations were the elements of
virtuosity; perhaps the folk of Sivishe enjoyed hints and
suggestions, fugitive lusters, almost unnoticeable inflec-
tions: their reaction to the Dirdir city so close at hand.

No less an index to the thought-processes of a
people was their religion. The Dirdir, so Reith knew
from conversations with Anacho, were irreligious. The
Dirdirmen, to the contrary, had evolved an elaborate
theology, based on a creation myth which derived Man
and Dirdir from a single primordial egg. The submen
of Sivishe patronized a dozen different temples. The
observances, as far as Reith could see, followed the
more or less universal pattern—abasement, followed by
a request for favors, as often as not foreknowledge re-

garding the outcome of the daily races. Certain cults had refined and complicated their doctrines; their doxology was a metaphysical jargon subtle and ambiguous enough to please even the folk of Sivishe. Other creeds serving different needs had simplified procedures so that the worshipers merely made a sacred sign, threw sequins into the priest's bowl, received a benediction and were off about their affairs.

The arrival of Woudiver's black car interrupted Reith's musing. Artilo, leaning forth with a leer, made a peremptory gesture, then sat crouched over the wheel staring off down the avenue.

The three entered the car, which lurched off across Sivishe. Artilo drove in a southeast direction, generally toward the spaceyards. At the edge of Sivishe, where a last few shacks dwindled out across the salt flats, a cluster of ramshackle warehouses surrounded piles of sand, gravel, bricks, sintered marl. The car rolled across the central compound and halted by a small office built of broken brick and black slag.

Woudiver stood in the doorway. Today he wore a vast brown jacket, blue pantaloons, and a blue hat. His expression was bland and unrevealing; his eyelids hung halfway across his eyes. He raised his arm in a gesture of measured welcome, then backed into the dimness of the hut. The three alighted and went within. Artilo, coming behind, drew himself a mug of tea from a great black urn, then, hissing irritably, went to sit in a corner.

Woudiver indicated a bench; the three seated themselves. Woudiver paced back and forth. He raised his face to the ceiling and spoke. "I have made a few casual inquiries. I fear that I find your project impractical. There is no difficulty as to work-space—the south warehouse yonder would suit admirably and you could have it at a reasonable rent. One of my trusted associates, the assistant superintendent of supply at the spaceyards, states that the necessary components are available . . . at a price. No doubt we could salvage a hull from the junk yard; you would hardly require luxury, and a crew of competent technicians would respond to a sufficiently attractive wage."

Reith began to suspect that Woudiver was leading up to something. "So, then, why is the project impractical?"

Woudiver smiled with innocent simplicity. "For me, the profit is inadequate to the risks involved."

Reith nodded somberly and rose to his feet. "I'm sorry then to have occupied so much of your time. Thank you very much for the information."

"Not at all," said Woudiver graciously. "I wish you the best of luck in your endeavor. Perhaps, when you return with your treasure, you will want to build a fine palace; then I hope you will remember me."

"Quite possibly," said Reith. "So now . . ."

Woudiver seemed in no hurry to have them go. He settled into a chair with an unctuous grunt. "Another dear friend deals in gems. He will efficiently convert your treasure into sequins, if the treasure is gems, as I presume? No? Rare metal, then? No? Aha! Precious essences?"

"It might be any or none," said Reith. "I think it best, at this stage, to remain indefinite."

Woudiver twisted his face into a mask of whimsical vexation. "It is precisely this indefiniteness which gives me pause! If I knew better what I might expect—"

"Whoever helps me," said Reith, "or whoever accompanies me, can expect wealth."

Woudiver pursed his lips. "So now I must join this piratical expedition in order to share the booty?"

"I'll pay a reasonable percentage before we leave. If you come with us"—Reith rolled his eyes toward the ceiling at the thought—"or when we return, you'll get more."

"How much more, precisely?"

"I don't like to say. You'd suspect me of irresponsibility. But you wouldn't be disappointed."

From the corner Artilo gave a skeptical croak, which Woudiver ignored. He spoke in a voice of great dignity. "As a practical man I can't operate on speculation. I would require a retaining fee of ten thousand sequins." He blew out his cheeks and glanced toward Reith. "Upon receipt of this sum, I would immediately exert my influence to set your scheme into motion."

"All very well," said Reith. "But, as a ridiculous supposition, let us assume that, rather than a man of honor, you were a scoundrel, a knave, a cheat. You might take my money, then find the project impossible for one reason or another, and I would have no recourse. Hence I can pay only for actual work accomplished."

A spasm of annoyance crossed Woudiver's face, but his voice was blandness itself. "Then pay me rent for yonder warehouse. It is a superb location, unobtrusive, close to the spaceyards, with every convenience. Furthermore I can obtain an old hull from the junk yards, purportedly for use as a storage bin. I will charge but a nominal rent, ten thousand sequins a year, payable in advance."

Reith nodded sagely. "An interesting proposition. But since we won't need the premises for more than a few months, why should we inconvenience you? We can rent more cheaply elsewhere, in even better circumstances."

Woudiver's eyes narrowed; the flaps of skin surrounding his mouth trembled. "Let us deal openly with each other. Our interests run together, as long as I gain sequins. I will not work on the cheap. Either pay earnest money, or our business is at an end."

"Very well," said Reith. "We will use your warehouse, and I will pay a thousand sequins for three months' rent on the day a suitable hull arrives on the premises and a crew starts to work."

"Hmf. That could be tomorrow."

"Excellent!"

"I will need funds to secure the hull. It has worth as scrap metal. Drayage will be a charge."

"Very well. Here is a thousand sequins." Reith counted the sum upon the desk. Woudiver slapped down his great slab of a hand. "Insufficient! Inadequate! Paltry!"

Reith spoke sharply. "Evidently you do not trust me. This does not predispose me to trust you. But you risk nothing but an hour or two of your time whereas I risk thousands of sequins."

Woudiver turned to Artilo. "What would you do?"

"Walk away from the mess."

Woudiver turned back to Reith, spread wide his arms. "There you have it."

Reith briskly picked up the thousand sequins. "Good day, then. It is a pleasure to have known you."

Neither Woudiver nor Artilo stirred.

The three returned to the hotel by public passenger wagon.

A day later Artilo appeared at the Ancient Realm Inn. "Aila Woudiver wants to see you."

"What for?"

"He's got you a hull. It's in the old warehouse. A gang is stripping and cleaning it. He wants money. What else?"

Chapter 13

The hull was satisfactory, and of adequate dimensions. The metal was sound; the observation ports were clouded and stained but well seated and sealed.

Woudiver stood to the side as Reith inspected the hull, an expression of lofty tolerance on his face. Every day, so it seemed, he wore a new and more extravagant garment, today a black and yellow suit, a black hat with a scarlet panache. The clasp securing his cape was a silver and black oval, bisected along the minor axis. From one end protruded the stylized head of a Dirdir, from the other the head of a man. Woudiver, noticing Reith's gaze, gave a profound nod. "You would never suspect as much from my physique, but my father was Immaculate."

"Indeed! And your mother?"

Woudiver's mouth twitched. "A noblewoman of the north."

Artilo spoke from the entry port: "A tavern wench of Thang, marsh-woman by blood."

Woudiver sighed. "In the presence of Artilo, romantic delusion is impossible. In any event, but for the accidental interposition of an incorrect womb, here would stand Aila Woudiver, Dirdirman Immaculate of the Violet Degree, rather than Aila Woudiver, dealer in sand and gravel, and gallant prosecutor of lost causes."

"Illogical," murmured Anacho. "In fact, improbable. Not one Immaculate in a thousand retains Primitive Paraphernalia."

Woudiver's face instantly became a peculiar magenta color. Whirling with astounding swiftness, he pointed a thick finger. "Who dares talk of logic and probability? The renegade Ankhe at afram Anacho! Who wore Blue and Pink without undergoing the Anguish? Who disappeared coincidentally with the Excellent Azarvim issit Dardo, who has never been seen again? A proud Dirdirman, this Ankhe at afram!"

"I no longer consider myself a Dirdirman," said Anacho in a level voice. "I definitely have no ambition for the Blue and Pink, nor even the trophies of my lineage."

"In this case kindly do not comment upon the plight of one who is unluckily barred from his rightful caste!"

Anacho turned away, fuming with anger, but obviously deeming it wise to hold his tongue. It appeared that Aila Woudiver had not been idle, and Reith wondered how far his researches had extended.

Woudiver gradually regained his composure. His mouth twitched, his cheeks puffed in and out. He made a scornful noise. "To more profitable matters. What is your opinion of this hulk?"

"Favorable," said Reith. "We could expect no better from the scrap-heap."

"This is my opinion as well," said Woudiver. "The next phase of course will be somewhat more difficult. My friend at the spaceyards is by no means anxious to run the Glass Box, no more I. But an adequacy of sequins works wonders. Which brings us to the subject of money. My out-of-pocket expenses are eight hundred and ninety sequins for the hull, which I consider good value. Drayage charge: three hundred sequins. Shop rental for one month: one thousand sequins. Total: twenty-one hundred and ninety sequins. My commission or personal profit I reckon at ten percent, or two hundred and nineteen sequins, to a total of twenty-four hundred and nine sequins."

"Wait, wait, wait!" cried Reith. "Not a thousand sequins a month, a thousand for *three* months; that was my offer."

"It is too little."

"I'll pay five hundred, not a clear more. Now in the matter of your commission, let us be reasonable. You provide drayage at a profit; I pay a large rent on your warehouse; I see no reason to hand over an additional ten percent on these items."

"Why not?" inquired Woudiver in a reasonable voice. "It is a convenience to you that I can offer these services. I wear two hats, so to speak: that of the expediter and that of the supplier. Why, merely because the expediter finds a certain supplier convenient, inexpensive and efficient, should he be denied his fee? If the drayage were performed elsewhere, the charges would be no less, and I would receive my fee without complaint."

Reith could not deny the logic of the presentation, nor did he try. He said, "I don't intend to pay more than five hundred sequins for a ramshackle old shed you'd be happy renting for two hundred."

Woudiver held up a yellow finger. "Consider the risk! We are about to suborn the thievery of valuable property! I am rewarded, please understand, partly for services rendered and partly to allay my fear of the Glass Box."

"This is a reasonable statement, from your point of view," said Reith. "As far as I am concerned, I want to complete the spaceship before the money runs out. After the ship is complete, fueled and provisioned, you can take every sequin remaining, for all I care."

"Indeed!" Woudiver scratched his chin. "How many sequins do you have then, so that we can plan accordingly?"

"Something over a hundred thousand."

"Mmf. I wonder if the job can be done at all—let alone allow for surplus."

"My point exactly. I want to keep non-construction expenses to the minimum."

Woudiver turned his face toward Artilo. "See how I am reduced. All prosper but Woudiver. As usual, he suffers for his generosity."

Artilo gave a noncommittal grunt.

Reith counted out sequins. "Five hundred—exorbitant rent for this ramshackle shed. Drayage: three hundred. The hull: eight hundred and ninety. I'll pay ten percent on the hull. Another eighty-nine. A total of seventeen hundred and seventy-nine."

Woudiver's broad yellow face mirrored a succession of emotions. At last he said, "I must remind you that a policy of parsimony is often the most expensive in the end."

"If the work goes efficiently," said Reith, "you won't find me parsimonious. You'll see more sequins than you ever dreamed existed. But I intend to pay only for results. It is to your interest to expedite the spaceboat as best you can. If the money runs out we're all the losers."

For once Woudiver had nothing to say. He stared dolefully at the glittering heap on the table, then, separating purples, scarlets, dark greens, he counted. "You drive a hard bargain."

"To our mutual benefit, ultimately."

Woudiver dropped the sequins into his pouch. "If I

must I must." He drummed his fingers against his thigh. "Well, as to the components, what do you require first?"

"I know nothing about Dirdir machinery. We need the advice of an expert technician. Such a man should be here now."

Woudiver squinted sidelong. "Without knowledge, how do you expect to fly?"

"I am acquainted with Wankh space-boats."

"Hmmf. Artilo, go fetch Deine Zarre from the Technical Club."

Woudiver stalked off to his office, leaving Reith, Anacho and Traz alone in the shed.

Anacho surveyed the hull. "The old shulk has done well. This is the Ispra, a series now obsolete, in favor of the Concax Screamer. We must obtain Ispra components, to simplify the work."

"Are these available?"

"Undoubtedly. I believe you got the better of the yellow beast. His father an Immaculate—what a joke! His mother a marsh-woman—that I can believe! He's evidently gone to pains to learn our secrets."

"I hope he doesn't learn too much."

"As long as we can pay, we're safe. We have a sound hull at a fair price, and even the rental is not too exorbitant. But we must be careful: normal profits won't suit him."

"No doubt he'll swindle us," said Reith. "If we end up with a functioning space-boat, I don't really care." He walked around the hull, occasionally reaching out to touch it, in a kind of wonder. Here, solid and definite, the basis of a vessel to take him home! Reith felt a surge of affection for the cold metal, in spite of its alien Dirdir look.

Traz and Anacho went outside to sit in the wan afternoon sunlight, and Reith presently joined them. With images of Earth in his mind, the landscape became suddenly strange, as if he were viewing it for the first time. The crumbling gray city Sivishe, the spires of

Hei, the Glass Box reflecting a dark bronze shine from Carina 4269, the loom of the Palisades through the murk: this was Tschai. He looked at Traz and Anacho: these were men of Tschai.

Reith sat down on the bench. He asked, "What's inside the Glass Box?"

Anacho seemed surprised at his ignorance. "It is a park, a simulation of old Sibol. Young Dirdir learn to hunt; others take exercise and relaxation. There are galleries for onlookers. Criminals are the prey. There are rocks, Sibol vegetation, cliffs, caves; sometimes a man avoids the hunt for days."

Reith looked across to the Glass Box. "The Dirdir hunt in there now?"

"So I suppose."

"What of the Dirdirmen Immaculates?"

"They are sometimes allowed to hunt."

"They devour their prey?"

"Of course."

Along the rutted road came the black car. It splashed through a puddle of oily slime, halted before the office. Woudiver came to stand in the doorway, a grotesque lump in black and yellow finery. Artilo stepped down from the driver's bench; from the cab came an old man. His face was haggard and his body seemed distorted or twisted; he moved slowly, as if every effort cost him pain. Woudiver strutted forward, spoke a word or two, then conducted the old man to the shed.

Woudiver spoke: "This is Deine Zarre, who will supervise our project. Deine Zarre, I introduce you to this man of no distinguishable race. He calls himself Adam Reith. Behind you see a defalcated Dirdirman: a certain Anacho; and a youth who appears to derive from the Kotan steppes. These are the folk with whom you must deal. I am no more than an adjunct; make all your arrangements with Adam Reith."

Deine Zarre gave his attention to Reith. His eyes were clear gray, and in contrast to the black of the pupils seemed almost luminious. "What is the project?"

Another man to know the secret, thought Reith. Already with Aila Woudiver and Artilo, the list was overlong. But no help for it. "In the shed is the hull of a space-boat. We want to put it into operative condition."

Deine Zarre's expression changed little. He searched Reith's face a moment, then turned and limped into the shed. Presently he reappeared. "The project is possible. Anything is possible. But feasible? I don't know." His gaze once more searched Reith's face. "There are risks."

"Woudiver shows no great alarm. Of all of us he is the most sensitive to danger."

Deine Zarre gave Woudiver a dispassionate glance. "He is also the most supple and resourceful. For myself, I fear nothing. If the Dirdir come to take me, I shall kill as many as possible."

"Come, come," chided Woudiver. "The Dirdir are as they are: folk of fantastic skills and courage. Are we not all Brothers of the Egg?"

Deine Zarre gave a dismal grunt. "Who is to supply machinery, tools, components?"

"The spaceyards," said Woudiver dryly. "Who else?"

"We will need technicians: at least six men, of absolute discretion."

"A chancy matter," Woudiver admitted. "But the chance can be minimized by inducements. If Reith pays them well, the inducement of money. If Artilo counsels them, the inducement of reason. If I indicate the consequences of a loose tongue, the inducement of fear. Never forget, Sivishe is a city of secrets! As witness we who stand here."

"True," said Deine Zarre. Again he searched Reith with his remarkable eyes. "Where do you wish to go in your spaceship?"

Woudiver spoke with overtones either of mockery or malice: "He goes to claim a fabulous treasure, which we all will share."

Deine Zarre smiled. "I want no treasure. Pay me a hundred sequins a week; it is all I require."

"So little?" demanded Woudiver. "You reduce my commission."

Deine Zarre gave him no heed. "You intend to start work at once?" he asked Reith.

"The sooner the better."

"I will list immediate needs." To Woudiver: "When can you arrange delivery?"

"As soon as Adam Reith provides the wherewithal."

"Put through the order tonight," said Reith. "I will bring money tomorrow."

"What of the honorarium for my friend?" demanded Woudiver testily. "Does he work for nothing? What of the fee for the warehouse guards? Do they look sideways for their health?"

"How much?" asked Reith.

Woudiver hesitated, then said in a dull voice, "Let us avoid a tiresome quarrel. I will present the minimum price first. Two thousand sequins."

"So much? Incredible. How many men must be bribed?"

"Three. The assistant supervisor, two guards."

Deine Zarre said, "Give it to him. I dislike haggling. If you must economize, pay me less."

Reith started to complain, then shrugged, managed a painful grin. "Very well. Two thousand sequins."

"Remember," said Woudiver, "you must bear the inventory cost of the merchandise; it is difficult to steal outright."

During the evening four power-wagons unloaded at the shed. Reith, Traz, Anacho and Artilo trundled the crates into the shed, as Deine Zarre checked them off his master list. Woudiver appeared on the scene at midnight. "All is well?"

Deine Zarre said, "As far as I can tell, the basic needs are here."

"Good." Woudiver turned to Reith, handed him a

sheet of paper. "The invoice. Notice that it is itemized, and bluster will serve no purpose."

Reith read the total in a weak whisper. "Eighty-two thousand sequins."

"Did you expect less?" Woudiver asked jauntily. "My fee is not included. Ninety thousand two hundred sequins in all."

Reith asked Deine Zarre, "Is this everything we need?"

"By no means."

"How much time will be required?"

"Two or three months. Longer if the components are seriously out of phase."

"What must I pay the technicians?"

"Two hundred sequins a week. Unlike myself, they are motivated by the need for money."

On the screen of Reith's imagination appeared a picture of the Carabas: the dun hills, the gray outcrops, the thickets of thorn, the horrid fires by night. He remembered the furtive passage across the Forelands, the Dirdir-trap in Boundary Forest, the race back to the Portal of Gleams. Ninety thousand sequins represented almost half of this. . . . If the money dwindled too fast, if Woudiver became too brazenly corrupt, what then? Reith could not bear to think the thought. "Tomorrow I will bring the money."

Woudiver gave a fateful nod. "Good. Or tomorrow night the goods return to the warehouse."

Chapter 14

Within the shed the old Ispra began to come alive. The propulsors were raised into their sockets, bolted and welded. Up through the stern access panel the generator and converter were hoisted, then slid forward and secured. The Ispra was no longer a hulk. Reith, Anacho and Traz wire-brushed, ground, polished, removed rotten padding, sour-smelling old settees. They cleaned the observation ports, reamed air conduits, installed new seals around the entry hatch.

Deine Zarre did no work. He hobbled here and there, his gray eyes missing no details. Artilo occasionally looked into the shed, a sneering droop to his gray mouth. Woudiver was seldom to be seen. During his rare appearances he was cold and businesslike, all trace of his first jocundity gone.

For an entire month Woudiver did not show himself. Artilo, in a confiding mood, spat down at the ground and said, "Big Yellow's out at his country place."

"Oh? What's he do out there?"

Artilo twisted his head sidewise, showing Reith a lopsided grin. "Thinks he's a Dirdirman, that's what. That's where his money goes, on his fences and scenery and hunts, wicked old beast."

Reith stood stock-still, staring at Artilo. "You mean he hunts men?"

"For sure. He and his cronies. Yellow has two thousand acres to his place, almost as big as the Glass Box. Walls aren't so good, but he's got them circled by electric wires and sting snaps. Don't go to sleep on Yellow's wine; you'll wake up to find yourself in the hunt."

Reith forebore to inquire the disposition of the victims; it was information he did not want.

Another of the ten-day Tschai weeks passed, and Woudiver appeared, in a surly mood. His upper lip was stiff as a shingle, totally concealing his mouth; his eyes darted truculently right and left. He strutted close to Reith; the great bulk of his torso blotted out half the landscape. He held out his hand. "Rent." His voice was flat and cold.

Reith brought forth five hundred sequins and placed them on a shelf. He did not care to touch the yellow hand.

Woudiver, in a spasm of petulance, struck out with the back of his hand, knocking Reith head over heels.

Reith picked himself up in astonishment. His skin began to prickle, signaling the onset of fury. From the corner of his eye he noticed Artilo lounging against the wall. Artilo would shoot him as calmly as he might crush an insect, this he knew. Nearby stood Traz, watching Artilo intently. Artilo was neutralized.

Woudiver stood looking at him, eyes cold and expressionless. Reith heaved a deep sigh, choked back his wrath. To strike back at Woudiver would gain none of his respect, but only stimulate the whole of his rancor. Inevitably something dreadful would occur. Reith slowly turned away. "Bring me my rent!" barked Woudiver. "Do you take me for a mendicant? I have been sufficiently wounded by your arrogance. In the future extend me the respect due to my caste!"

Again Reith hesitated. How much easier to attack the monstrous Woudiver and accept the consequences! Which would be wreckage of the program. Again Reith sighed. If it were necessary to eat crow, a mouthful was no worse than a taste.

In cold and austere silence he handed the sequins to Woudiver, who only glared and made a waggling motion of the hips. "It is insufficient! Why should I subsidize your undertaking! Pay me my due! The rent is one thousand sequins a month!"

"Here is another five hundred sequins," said Reith. "Please do not demand more, because it will not be forthcoming."

Woudiver made a contemptuous sound, wheeled and stalked away. Artilo looked after him and spat in the dust. Then he gave Reith a speculative glance.

Reith want inside the shed. Deine Zarre, who had observed the episode, made no comment. Reith tried to soothe his humiliation in work.

Two days later Woudiver reappeared, wearing his gaudy black and yellow outfit. His truculence of the previous occasion had vanished; he was blandly polite. "Well, then, and what is the current state of your project?"

Reith responded in a flat voice. "There have been no major problems. The heavy components are in place and connected. The instruments have been installed, but are not operative. Deine Zarre is preparing another list: the magnetic justification system, navigation sensors, the environment conditioners. Perhaps we should also purchase fuel cells at this time."

Woudiver pursed his lips. "Just so. Again the sad occasion arises, of parting with your hard-gained sequins. How, may I ask, did you garner so large a sum? It is a fortune in itself. With so much in hand I wonder that you risk all on a wild-goose chase."

Reith managed a wintry smile. "Evidently I do not regard the expedition as a wild-goose chase."

"Extraordinary. When will Deine Zarre have his list in hand?"

"Perhaps it is finished now."

Deine Zarre had not finished his list but did so while Woudiver waited.

Scanning the list with head thrown back and eyes half-closed, Woudiver said, "I fear that the expense will be in excess of your reserves."

"I hope not," said Reith. "How much do you reckon?"

"I can't say for certain; I do not know. But with rent, labor costs, your original investments, you cannot have too much money left." He looked at Reith questioningly.

The last thing Reith planned to do was confide in Woudiver. "It is essential then that we keep costs to a minimum."

"Three basic costs must be met without fail," intoned Woudiver. "The rent, my fees, honorariums to my associates. What remains may be spent as you will. This is my point of view. And now be so good as to tender me two thousand sequins, for the honorariums. The materials, should you be unable to pay, can be returned without prejudice and at no cost other than drayage fees."

Gloomily Reith handed over two thousand sequins.

He made a mental calculation: of something like two hundred and twenty thousand sequins brought from the Carabas, less than half remained.

During the night three power-wagons brought goods to the shed.

Somewhat later a smaller wagon arrived, with eight canisters of fuel. Traz and Anacho started to unload these, but Reith stopped them. "One moment." He went into the shed where Deine Zarre checked items off his list. "Did you order fuel?"

"Yes."

Deine Zarre seemed pensive, thought Reith, as if his mind wandered afield.

"How long will a canister of fuel drive the shop?"

"Two are needed, one for each cell. These will give about two months' service."

"Eight canisters have been delivered."

"I ordered four, to ensure two spares."

Reith returned to the dray. "Take off four," he told Traz and Anacho. The driver sat in the shadow of the cab. Reith leaned in to address him, and to his surprise saw Artilo, apparently in no anxiety to identify himself. Reith said, "You brought eight cans of fuel; we ordered four."

"Yellow said to bring eight."

"We only need four. Take four back."

"Can't be done. Talk to Big Yellow."

"I need only four cans. That's all I'm taking. Do what you like with the others."

Artilo, whistling between his teeth, jumped from the cab, unloaded the four extra canisters, carried them over to the shed. Then he climbed back into the dray and drove off.

The three stood looking after him. Anacho said in a toneless voice, "Trouble is on its way."

"I expect so," said Reith.

"The fuel cells," said Anacho, "are no doubt Woudiver's own property. Perhaps he stole them, perhaps he bought them on the cheap. Here is an excellent chance to dispose of them at a profit."

Traz made a growling sound in his throat. "Woudiver should be made to carry away the cells on his back."

Reith gave an uneasy laugh. "If I only knew how to make him."

"He fears for his life, like anyone else."

"True. But we can't cut off our nose to spite our face."

In the morning Woudiver did not arrive to hear the statements which Reith had brooded upon a large part of the night. Reith drove himself to work, with the thought of Woudiver pressing on him like the weight of doom.

On this morning Deine Zarre was not on hand either, and the technicians muttered among themselves more freely than they dared in Deine Zarre's presence. Reith presently desisted from his work and made a survey of the project. There were, he thought, good grounds for optimism. The major components were installed; the delicate job of tuning proceeded at a satisfactory rate. At these jobs Reith, though acquainted with Earth space-drive systems, was helpless. He was not even certain that the drives functioned by the same principles.

About noon a line of black clouds broke over the palisades like a scud of surf. Carina 4269 went wan, faded through tones of brown and disappeared; moments later rain swept the eerie landscape, blotting Hei from sight, and now plodding through the rain came Deine Zarre, followed by a pair of thin children: a boy of twelve, a girl three or four years older. The three trudged into the shed, where they stood shivering. Deine Zarre seemed drained of energy; the children were numb.

Reith broke up some crates, lit a fire in the middle of the shed. He found some coarse cloth and tore it into towels. "Dry yourselves. Take off your jackets and get warm."

Deine Zarre looked at him uncomprehendingly, then slowly obeyed. The children followed suit. They were evidently brother and sister, quite possibly Deine Zarre's grandchildren. The boy's eyes were blue; those of the girl were a beautiful slate gray.

Reith brought forth hot tea and at last Deine Zarre spoke. "Thank you. We are almost dry." And a moment later: "The children are in my care; they will be with me. If you find the prospect inconvenient, I must give up my employment."

"Of course not," said Reith. "They are welcome here, as long as they understand the need for silence."

"They will say nothing." Deine Zarre looked at the two. "Do you understand? Whatever you see must not be mentioned elsewhere."

The three were in no mood for conversation. Reith, sensing desolation and misery, lingered. The children watched him warily. "I can't offer you dry clothes," said Reith. "But are you hungry? We have food on hand."

The boy shook his head with dignity; the girl smiled and became suddenly charming. "We have had no breakfast."

Traz, who had been standing to the side, ran to the larder and presently returned with seed-bread and soup. Reith watched gravely. It appeared that Traz's emotions had been affected. The girl was appealing, if somewhat peaked and miserable.

Deine Zarre finally stirred himself. He pulled his steaming garments taut and went to inspect the work done in his absence.

Reith tried to make conversation with the children. "Are you becoming dry?"

"Yes, thank you."

"Deine Zarre is your grandfather?"

"Our uncle."

"I see. And now you are to live with him?"

"Yes."

Reith could find nothing more to say. Traz was more direct. "What happened to your father and mother?"

"They were killed, by Fairos," said the girl softly. The boy blinked.

Anacho said, "You must be from the Eastern Skyrise."

"Yes."

"How did you get from there to here?"

"We walked."

"It is a long way, and dangerous."

"We were lucky." The two stared into the fire. The girl winced, recalling the circumstances of their flight.

Reith went off to find Deine Zarre. "You have new responsibilities."

Deine Zarre darted Reith a sharp look. "That is correct."

"You work here for less than you deserve to be paid, and I want to increase your salary."

Deine Zarre gave a gruff nod. "I can put the money to use."

Reith returned to the floor of the shed, to find Woudiver standing in the doorway, a vast bulbous silhouette. His attitude was one of shocked disapproval. Today he wore another of his grand outfits: black plush breeches tight around his massive legs, a coat of purple and brown with a dull yellow sash. He marched forward to stare fixedly down at the boy and the girl, one to the other. "Who built this fire? What do you do here?"

The girl quavered: "We were wet; the gentleman warmed us before the fire."

"Aha. And who is this gentleman?"

Reith came forward. "I am the gentleman. These are relatives of Deine Zarre. I built the fire to dry them."

"What of my property? A single spark and all goes up in flames!"

"In the rain I conceived the danger to be slight."

Woudiver made an easy gesture. "I accept your reassurances. How does all proceed?"

"Well enough," said Reith.

Woudiver reached into his sleeve and brought forth a paper. "I have here an account for the deliveries of last night. The total, you will notice, is extremely low, because I was given an inclusive lot price."

Reith unfolded the paper. Black sprawling characters spelled out: *Merchandise, as supplied: Sequins 106,800.*

Woudiver was saying: "—appears we are proceeding in really wonderful luck. I hope it will last. Only yesterday the Dirdir trapped two thieves working out of the export warehouse and took them instantly to the Glass Box. So, you see, our present security is fragile."

"Woudiver," said Reith, "this bill is too high. Far too high. Further, I don't intend to pay for extra energy-cans."

"The price, as I noted," said Woudiver, "is an inclusive one. The extra cans come at no extra cost. In a sense, they are free."

"This is not the case, and I refuse to pay five times what is reasonable. In fact, I don't have enough money."

"Then you must get some more," said Woudiver softly.

Reith snorted. "You make the task sound so easy."

"It is for some," said Woudiver airily. "A most remarkable rumor circulates the city. It appears that three men, entering the Carabas, slaughtered an astonishing number of Dirdir, subsequently robbing the bodies. The men are described as a youth, fair, like a Kotan steppe-dweller; a renegade Dirdirman; and a dark quiet man of no distinguishable race. The Dirdir are anxious to hunt down these three. Another rumor purports to concern the same three men. The dark man reportedly states his origin to be a faroff world from which he insists all men derive: in my opinion a blasphemy. What do you think of all this?"

"Interesting," said Reith, trying to conceal his despair.

Woudiver permitted himself to smirk. "We are in a vulnerable position. There is danger to myself, grave danger. Should I expose myself for nothing? I assist you from motives of comradeship and altruism of course, but I must receive my recompense."

"I cannot pay so much," said Reith. "You knew approximately the extent of my capital; now you attempt to extort more."

"Why not?" Woudiver could no longer restrain a grin. "Assume that the rumors I cited are accurate; assume that by some wild accident you and your henchmen were the persons in question: then is it not true that you have shamefully deceived me?"

"Assuming as much—not at all."

"What of the wonderful treasure?"

"It is real. Assist me to the best of your abilities. In one month we can depart Tschai. In another month you will be repaid beyond your dreams."

"Where? How?" Woudiver hitched himself forward; he loomed over Reith and his voice came deep and rich from the far caverns of his chest. "Let me ask outright: did you promulgate a tale that the original home of man is a far world? Or even more to the point: do you believe this hideous fantasy?"

Reith, with spirits plunging even deeper, tried to sidestep the quagmire. "We are dealing with side issues. Our arrangement was clear; the rumors you mention have no relevance."

Woudiver slowly, deliberately, shook his head.

"When the spaceship leaves," said Reith, "you shall have every sequin in my possession. I can do no better than that. If you make unreasonable demands . . ." He searched for a convincing threat.

Woudiver tilted up the great expanse of his face, chuckled. "What can you do? You are helpless. One word from me and you are instantly taken to the Glass Box. What are your options? None. You must do as I demand."

Reith looked around the shed. In the doorway stood Artilo, applying ash-gray snuff to his nostrils. At his belt hung a hand-gun.

Deine Zarre approached. Ignoring Woudiver he spoke to Reith. "The energy-cans are not to my order. They are a non-standard size and appear to have been used for an indeterminate period. They must be rejected."

Wouldiver's eyes narrowed, his mouth jerked. "What? They are excellent canisters."

Deine Zarre said in a toneless but utterly definite voice, "For our purposes they are useless." He departed. The boy and the girl looked after him wistfully. Wouldiver turned to examine them, with what appeared to Reith a peculiar intensity.

Reith waited. Wouldiver swung about. For a moment he regarded Reith through narrow-lidded eyes. "Well, then," said Wouldiver, "it seems that different energy-cans are needed. How do you propose to pay for them?"

"In the usual way. Take back those eight cans of junk; provide four fresh cans and submit an itemized bill. A fair account I am able to pay—just barely. Don't forget, I must meet labor costs."

Wouldiver considered. Deine Zarre crossed the shed to speak to the boy and girl and Wouldiver was distracted. He strutted over to join the group. Reith, limp with fatigue, went to the workbench and poured himself a mug of tea, which he drank with a shaking hand.

Wouldiver had become extremely affable, and went so far as to pat the boy on the head. Deine Zarre stood stiff, his face the color of wax.

Wouldiver at last turned away. He crossed the shed to Artilo, spoke a moment or two. Artilo went outside, where blasts of wind sent ripples scurrying across the puddles.

Wouldiver signaled Reith with one hand, Deine Zarre with the other. The two approached. Wouldiver sighed with vast melancholy. "You two are dedicated to my poverty. You insist on the most exquisite refinements but refuse to pay. So be it. Artilo is taking away the canisters you so condemn. Zarre, come with me now and select cells to suit your needs."

"At this moment? I must take care of the two children."

"Now, at once. Tonight I visit my little property. I will not return for a period. It is evident that my help is undervalued here."

Deine Zarre acquiesced with poor grace. He spoke to the boy and the girl, then departed with Woudiver.

Two hours passed. The sun, breaking through the clouds, sent a single ray down upon Hei, so that the scarlet and purple towers glittered against the black sky. Down the road came Woudiver's black car. It rolled to a halt in front of the shed; Artilo alighted. He sauntered into the shed. Reith watched him, wondering as to his air of purposefulness. Artilo approached the boy and girl, stood looking down at them, and they in turn looked up, eyes wide in their pale faces. Artilo spoke a few terse words; Reith could see the corded muscles at the back of his jaw jerk as he spoke. The children looked dubiously across the room at Reith, then reluctantly started to move toward the door. Traz spoke to Reith in a low urgent voice: "Something is wrong. What does he want with them?"

Reith moved forward. He asked, "Where are you taking these two?"

"No affair of yours."

Reith turned to the children. "Don't go with this man. Wait until your uncle returns."

The girl said, "He says he is taking us to our uncle."

"He can't be believed. Something is wrong."

Artilo turned to face Reith, an act as sinister as the coiling of a snake. He spoke in a soft voice. "I have my orders. Stand away."

"Who gave you the orders? Woudiver?"

"It is no concern of yours." He motioned to the two children. "Come." His hand went under his old gray jacket and he watched Reith sidelong.

The girl said, "We are not going with you."

"You must. I'll carry you."

"Touch them and I'll kill you," said Reith in a flat voice.

Artilo gave him a cool stare. Reith braced himself, muscles creaking with tension. Artilo brought forth his hand; Reith saw the dark shape of a weapon. He lunged, chopped down at the cold hard arm. Artilo had been expecting this; from the sleeve of his other hand sprang a long blade, which he thrust at Reith's side, so swiftly that Reith, whirling away, felt the sting of the edge. Artilo sprang back, knife poised, though he had lost the hand-gun. Reith, intoxicated with fury and the sudden release of tension, edged forward, eyes fixed on the unblinking Artilo. Reith feinted. Artilo reacted by not so much as a quiver. Reith struck with his left hand; Artilo cut up; Reith seized his wrist, whirled, bent, heaved, threw him far across the room where he lay in a crumpled heap.

Reith dragged him to the door, threw him outside into a puddle of slime.

Artilo painfully hoisted himself to his feet and limped over to the black car. In a passionless matter-of-fact fashion, never looking toward the shed, he scraped the mud from his garments, entered the car and departed.

Anacho said in a disapproving voice, "You should have killed him. Matters will be worse than ever."

Reith had no reply to make. He became conscious of the blood oozing down his side. Pulling up his shirt he found a long thin slash. Traz and Anacho applied a dressing; the girl somewhat timidly approached and tried to help. She seemed deft and capable; Anacho moved aside. Traz and the girl completed the job.

"Thank you," said Reith.

The girl looked up at him, her face full of a hundred different meanings. But she could not bring herself to speak.

The afternoon waned. The girl and boy stood in the doorway looking up the road. The technicians departed; the shed was silent.

The black car returned. Deine Zarre stepped stiffly forth, followed by Woudiver. Artilo, going to the luggage compartment, brought forth four energy cells, which he carried at a painful hobble into the shed. His manner, as far as Reith could see, was no different from usual: dour, impersonal, silent.

Woudiver turned a single glance toward the girl and

the boy, who shrank back into the shadows. Then he approached Reith. "The energy canisters are here. They are approved by Zarre. They cost a great deal of money. Here is my statement for next month's rent and Artilo's salary—"

"Artilo's salary?" demanded Reith. "You must be joking."

"—the total, as you see, is exactly one hundred thousand sequins. The sum is not subject to diminution. You must pay at once or I will evict you from the premises." And Woudiver pursed his lips in a cold smile.

Reith's eyes misted with hate. "I can't afford this amount of money."

"Then you must go. Further, since you are no longer my client, I will be obligated to make a report of your activities to the Dirdir."

Reith nodded. "One hundred thousand sequins. And after that, how much more?"

"Whatever sums you require me to lay out."

"No further blackmail?"

Woudiver drew himself up. "The word is capricious and vulgar. I warn you, Adam Reith, that I expect the same courtesy that I accord."

Reith managed a sad laugh. "You'll have your money in five or six days. I don't have it now."

Woudiver cocked his great head skeptically sidewise. "Where do you propose to secure this money?"

"I have money waiting for me in Coad."

Woudiver snorted, wheeled and marched to his car. Artilo hobbled after him. They departed.

Traz and Anacho came to watch after the car.

In a wondering voice Traz asked, "Where will you get a hundred thousand sequins?"

"We left as much buried in the Carabas," said Reith. "The only problem is bringing it back—and perhaps it won't be so much of a problem after all."

Anacho's lank white jaw dropped. "I've always suspected you of insane optimism . . ."

Reith held up his hand. "Listen. I will fly north by

the same route the Dirdir themselves use. They will take no notice, even should a search-screen be operating, which is doubtful. I will land after dark, to the east of the forest. In the morning I will dig up the sequins and take them back to the sky-car and at dusk I will fly back to Sivishe like a party of Dirdir returning from the hunt."

Anacho gave a derogatory grunt. "You make it sound so simple."

"As probably it will be, if all goes well."

Reith looked wistfully back toward the shed and the half-complete spaceship. "I might as well start now."

"I'll go with you," said Traz. "You'll need help."

Anacho made a dreary sound. "I had better go as well."

Reith shook his head. "One can do the job as well as three. You two remain here and keep our affairs moving."

"And if you don't return?"

"There are sixty or seventy thousand sequins still in the pouch. Take the money and leave Sivishe. . . . But I'll be back. I can't doubt this. It's not possible that we should toil and suffer so greatly only to fail."

"Hardly a rational assessment," Anacho said dryly. "I expect never to see you again."

"Nonsense," said Reith. "Well, I'll get started. The sooner I leave, the sooner I return."

Chapter 15

The sky-car sailed quietly through the night of old Tschai, over landscape ghostly in the light of the blue moon. Reith felt like a man drifting through a strange dream. He mused over the events of his life—his childhood, his years of training, his missions among the

stars and finally his assignment to the *Explorator IV*.
Then Tschai: destruction and disaster, his time with
the Emblem nomads, the journey across Aman Steppe
and the Dead Steppe to Pera; the sack of Dadiche; the
subsequent journey to Cath and his adventures at Ao
Hidis. Then the journey to Carabas, the slaughter of
the Dirdir, the construction of the spaceship in Sivishe.
And Woudiver! On Tschai both virtue and vice were
exaggerated; Reith had known many evil men, among
whom Woudiver ranked high.

The night advanced; the forests of central Kislovan
gave way to barren uplands and silent wasteland. In all
the circle of vision, no light, no fire, no sign of human
activity was visible. Reith consulted the course monitor, adjusted the automatic pilot. The Carabas lay only
an hour ahead. The blue moon hung low; when it set
the landscape would be dark until dawn.

The hour passed. Braz sank behind the horizon; in
the east appeared a sepia glimmer announcing the
nearness of dawn. Reith, dividing his attention between
the course monitor and the ground below, finally
thought to glimpse the shape of Khusz. At once he
dropped the car low to the ground and veered to the
east, swinging behind the Boundary Forest. As Carina
4269 thrust a first cool brown sliver over the edge of
the horizon Reith landed, close under the first great
torquils of the forest.

For a period he sat watching and listening. Carina
4269 rose into the sky and the low light shone directly
upon the sky-car. Reith gathered broken fronds and
branches, which he lay against the car, camouflaging it
to some extent.

The time had come when he must venture into the
forest. He could delay no longer. Taking a sack and a
shovel, tucking weapons into his belt, Reith set forth.

The trail was familiar. Reith recognized each bole,
every dark sheaf of fungus, every hummock of lichen.
As he passed through the forest he became aware of a
sickening odor: the reek of carrion. This was to be ex-

pected. He halted. Voices? Reith jumped off the trail, listened.

Voices indeed. Reith hesitated, then stole forward through the heavy foliage.

Ahead lay the site of the trap. Reith approached with the most extreme caution, creeping on his hands and knees, finally crawling on his elbows. . . . He looked forth upon an eerie sight. To one side, in front of a great torquil, stood five Dirdir in hunting regalia. A dozen gray-faced men stood in a great hole, digging with shovels and buckets: this was the hole, greatly enlarged, in which Reith, Traz and Anacho had buried the Dirdir corpses. From the splendid rotting carrion came an odious stench. . . . Reith stared. One of these men was surely familiar—it was Issam the Thang. And next to him worked the hostler, and next, the porter at the Alawan. The others Reith could not positively identify, but all seemed somehow familiar, and he assumed them to be folk with whom he had dealings at Maust.

Reith turned to inspect the five Dirdir. They stood stiff and attentive, effulgences flaring out behind. If they felt emotion, or disgust, none was evident.

Reith did not allow himself to reason, to weigh, to calculate. He brought forth his hand-gun; he aimed, he fired. Once, twice, three times. The Dirdir fell dead; the other two sprang around in questioning fury. Four times, five times: two glancing hits. Emerging from his covert Reith fired twice more down into the thrashing white bodies before they became still.

The men in the pit stood frozen in wonder. "Up!" cried Reith. "Out of there!"

Issam the Thang yelled hoarsely, "It is you, the murderer! Your crimes brought us here!"

"Never mind that," said Reith. "Get up out of that hole and fly for your life!"

"What good is that? The Dirdir will track us! They will kill us in some abominable fashion—"

The hostler was already out of the hole. He went to the Dirdir corpses, availed himself of a weapon, and turned back to Issam the Thang. "Don't bother to climb from the hole." He fired; the Thang's yell was cut short; his body rolled down among the decaying Dirdir.

The hostler said to Reith, "He betrayed us all, hoping for gain; he gained only what you saw; they took him with the rest of us."

"These five Dirdir—were there more?"

"Two Excellences who have gone back to Khusz."

"Take the weapons and go your way."

The men fled toward the Hills of Recall. Reith dug under the roots of the torquil. There, the sack of sequins. To the value of a hundred thousand? He could not be sure.

Shouldering the pouch, looking for a last time on the scene of carnage and the pitiful corpse of Issam the Thang, he departed the scene.

Back at the sky-car he loaded the sequins into the cabin and set himself to wait, anxiety gnawing at his stomach. He dared not depart. If he flew low he might be seen by hunt parties; if he flew high the screen across the Carabas would detect him.

The day passed. Carina 4269 dropped behind the far hills. Sad brown twilight fell over the Zone. Along the hills the hateful flickers sprang into existence. Reith could wait no longer. He took the sky-car into the air.

Low over the ground he skimmed until he was clear of the Zone, then rising high drove south for Sivishe.

Chapter 16

The dark land passed astern. Reith sat staring ahead, visions flitting across his inner eye: faces, twisted in passion, horror, pain. The shapes of Blue Chasch, Wankh, Pnume, Phung, Green Chasch, Dirdir, all leaped upon the stage of his imagination, to stand, turn, perform a gesture and leap away.

The night passed. The sky-car slid south and when Carina 4269 rose into the east the spires of Hei glistened far ahead.

Without incident Reith landed the sky-car, though it seemed that a passing party of Dirdirmen scrutinized him with suspicious intensity as he departed the field with his sack of sequins.

Reith went first to his room at the Ancient Realm. Neither Traz nor Anacho was on the premises, but Reith thought nothing of this; they often passed nights at the shed.

Reith stumbled to his couch, threw the bag of sequins against the wall, stretched out and almost immediately slept.

He awoke to a hand on his shoulder. He rolled over to find Traz standing above him.

Traz spoke in a husky voice: "I was afraid you'd come here. Hurry, we must leave. The apartment is now dangerous."

Reith, still torpid, swung himself to a sitting position. The time was early afternoon, or so he judged by the shadows outside the window.

"What's the trouble?"

"The Dirdir took Anacho into custody. I was out buying food, or they would have taken me as well."

Reith was now fully awake. "When did this happen?"

"Yesterday. It was Woudiver's doing. He came to the shed, and asked questions about you. He wanted to know if you claimed to come from another world; he persisted and would not accept evasion. I refused to speak, as did Anacho. Woudiver began to reproach Anacho as a renegade. 'You, a former Dirdirman, how can you live like a subman among submen?' Anacho became provoked and said that Bifold Genesis was a myth. Woudiver went away. Yesterday morning the Dirdir came here to the rooms and took Anacho. If they force him to talk, we are not safe and the ship is not safe."

Reith's fingers were numb as he pulled on his boots. All at once the structure of his life, contrived at such cost, had collapsed. Woudiver, always Woudiver.

Traz touched his arm. "Come; best that we leave! The rooms may be watched."

Reith picked up the bundle of sequins. They departed the building. Through the alleys of Sivishe they walked, ignoring the pale faces looking forth from doorways and odd-shaped windows.

Reith became aware that he was ravenously hungry; at a small restaurant they ate boiled sea-thrush and spore-cake. Reith began to think more clearly. Anacho was in Dirdir custody; Woudiver would certainly be expecting some sort of reaction from him. Or would he be so assured of Reith's essential helplessness that he would expect matters to go on as before? Reith grinned a ghastly grin. If Woudiver reckoned as much, he would be right. Unthinkable to jeopardize the ship for any circumstance whatever! Reith's hate for Woudiver was like a tumor in his brain—and he must ignore it; he must make the best of an agonizing dilemma.

Reith asked Traz, "You have not seen Woudiver?"

"I saw him this morning. I went to the shed; I thought you might have gone there. Woudiver arrived and went into his office."

"Let's see if he's still there."

"What do you intend to do?"

Reith gave a strangled laugh. "I could kill him—but it would do no good. We need information. Woudiver is the only source."

Traz said nothing; as usual Reith was unable to read his thoughts.

They rode the creaking six-wheeled public carrier out to the construction yard, and every turn of the wheels wound the tension tighter. When Reith arrived at the yard and saw Woudiver's black car the blood surged through his brain and he felt light-headed. He stood still, drew a deep breath and became quite calm.

He thrust the pouch of sequins upon Traz. "Take it into the shed and hide it."

Traz took the sack dubiously. "Don't go alone. Wait for me."

"I expect no trouble. We can't afford the luxury, as Woudiver well knows. Wait for me by the shed."

Reith went to Woudiver's eccentric stone office and entered. With his back to a charcoal brazier stood Artilo, legs splayed, arms behind his back. He examined Reith without change of expression.

"Tell Woudiver I want to see him," said Reith.

Artilo sauntered to the inner door, thrust his head in, spoke. He backed away. The door swung aside with a wrench that almost tore it from its hinges. Woudiver expanded into the room: a glaring-eyed Woudiver with great upper lip folded down over his mouth. He looked across the room with the unfocused all-seeing glare of a wrathful god, then seemed to catch sight of Reith, and his malevolence concentrated itself.

"Adam Reith," spoke Woudiver in a voice like a bell. "You have returned. Where are my sequins?"

"Never mind your sequins," said Reith. "Where is the Dirdirman?"

Woudiver hunched his shoulders. For a moment Reith thought that he was about to strike out. If so Reith knew that his self-control would dissolve, for better or worse.

Woudiver spoke in a throbbing voice: "Do you think to fatigue me with wrangling? Think again! Give me my money and depart."

"You shall have your money," said Reith, "as soon as I see Ankhe at afram Anacho."

"You wish to see the blasphemer, the renegade?" roared Woudiver. "Go to the Glass Box; you will see him clearly enough."

"He is in the Glass Box?"

"Where else?"

"You are certain?"

Woudiver leaned back against the wall. "Why do you wish to know?"

"Because he is my friend. You betrayed him to the Dirdir; you must answer to me."

Woudiver began to swell, but Reith said in a weary voice, "No more drama, no more shouting. You gave Anacho to the Dirdir; now I want you to save him."

"Impossible," said Woudiver. "Even if I wished, I could do nothing. He is in the Glass Box, do you hear?"

"How can you be sure?"

"Where else should he be sent? He was taken for his old crimes; the Dirdir will learn nothing of your project, if that is your worry." And Woudiver showed his mouth in a gigantic sneer. "Unless, of course, he himself reveals your secrets."

"In which case," said Reith, "you would likewise find yourself in difficulties."

Woudiver had no comment to make.

Reith asked in a gentle voice, "Can money buy Anacho's escape?"

"No," intoned Woudiver. "He is in the Glass Box."

"So you say. How can I be sure?"

"As I informed you—go look."

"Anyone who wishes can watch?"

"Certainly. The Box holds no secrets."

"What is the procedure?"

"You cross to Hei, you walk to the Box, you climb to the upper gallery which overlooks the field."

"Could a person lower a rope, or a ladder?"

"Certainly, but he could not hope for long life; he would be thrust at once down upon the field. . . . If you plan anything of this nature I myself will come to watch."

"Suppose I were to offer you a million sequins," said Reith, "could you arrange that Anacho escape?"

Woudiver darted his great head forward. "A million sequins? And you have been crying poverty to me for three months? I have been been deceived!"

"Could you arrange the escape for a million sequins?"

Woudiver showed a dainty pink tip of tongue. "No, I

fear not . . . a million sequins . . . I fear not. There is
nothing to be done. Nothing. So you have gained a million sequins?"

"No," said Reith. "I only wanted to learn if Anacho's escape was possible."

"It is not possible," said Woudiver crossly. "Where
is my money?"

"In due course," said Reith. "You betrayed my
friend; you can wait."

Again Woudiver seemed on the verge of swinging his
great arm. But he said, "You misuse language. I did
not 'betray'; I exposed a criminal to his just deserts.
What loyalty do I owe you or yours? You have given
none to me, and would do worse if opportunity offered.
Bear in mind, Adam Reith, that friendship must work
in two directions. Do not expect what you are unwilling
to give. If you find my attributes distasteful, remember
that I feel the same about yours. Which of us is correct? By the standards of this time and this place, it is
certainly I. You are the interloper; your protests are lu-
dicrous and unrealistic. You blame me for inordinacy.
Do not forget, Adam Reith, that you chose me as a
man who would perform illegal acts for pay. This is
your expectation of me; you care nothing for my security or prospects. You came here to exploit me, to
urge me to dangerous acts for trifling sums; you must
not complain if my conduct seems merely a mirror of
your own."

Reith could find no answer. He turned and left the
office.

In the shed work was proceeding at its usual pace: a
haven of normalcy after the Carabas and the mind-
twisting colloquy with Woudiver. Traz waited just inside the portal. "What did he say?"

"He said Anacho was a criminal, that I came here to
exploit him. How can I argue?"

Traz curled his lip. "And Anacho?"

"In the Glass Box. Woudiver says it's easy to get in
but impossible to get out." Reith walked back and
forth across the shed. Halting in the doorway, he

looked across the water toward the great gray shape. He spoke to Traz: "Will you ask Deine Zarre to step out here?"

Deine Zarre appeared. Reith asked, "Have you ever visited the Glass Box?"

"Long ago."

"Woudiver tells me that a man might lower a rope from the upper gallery."

"Should he care so little for his life."

"I want two quantities of high-potency battarache—enough, say, to destroy this shed ten times over. Where can I get it in a hurry?"

Deine Zarre reflected a moment, then gave a slow fateful nod. "Wait here."

He returned in something over an hour with two clay pots. "Here is battarache; here are fuses. It is contraband material; please do not reveal where you obtained it."

"The subject will never arise," said Reith. "Or so I hope."

Chapter 17

Shrouded in gray cloaks Reith and Traz crossed the causeway to the mainland. By a fine wide avenue, surfaced with a rough white substance that rasped underfoot, they entered the Dirdir city Hei. To either hand rose spires, purple and scarlet; those of gray metal and silver stood far to the north behind the Glass Box. The avenue led close beside a hundred-foot shaft of scarlet. Surrounding this was an expanse of clean white sand upon which rested a dozen peculiar objects of polished stone. Art-things? Fetishes? Trophies? There was no way of knowing. In front of the spire, on a circular plat of white marble, stood three Dirdir. For the first time

Reith saw a Dirdir female. The creature was shorter and seemed less resilient, less flexible, than the male; her head was wider at the scalp and pointed at the area corresponding to a chin; she was somewhat darker in color: a pallid gray subtly shaded with mauve. The two stood contemplating the third, a male Dirdir whelp, half the size of the adult. From time to time the effulgences of the three twitched to point to one or another of the polished rock-pieces, an activity which Reith made no effort to understand.

Reith watched them in a mingling of revulsion and reluctant admiration, and he could not avoid thinking of the "mysteries."

Some time previously Anacho had explained the Dirdir sexual processes. "Essentially, the facts are these: there are twelve styles of male sexual organs, fourteen of the female. Only certain pairings are possible. For instance, the Type One Male is compatible only with Types Five and Nine Female. Type Five Female adjusts only to Type One Male, but Type Nine Female has a more general organ and is compatible with Types One, Eleven and Twelve Male.

"The matter becomes fantastically complex. Each male and female style has its specific name and theoretical attributes, which are very seldom realized—as long as an individual's type is secret! These are the Dirdir 'mysteries'! Should an individual's type become known, he is expected to conform to the theoretical attributes of the type, regardless of inclination; he rarely does so, and is constantly embarrassed on this account.

"As you can imagine, a matter so complicated absorbs a great deal of attention and energy and, perhaps, by keeping the Dirdir fragmented, obsessed and secretive, has prevented them from overrunning the worlds of space."

"Amazing," said Reith. "But if the types are secret and generally incompatible, how do they mate? How do they reproduce?"

"There are several systems: trial marriage, the so-

called 'dark gatherings,' anonymous notices. The difficulties are transcended." Anacho paused a moment,
then proceeded delicately. "I need hardly point out
that low-caste Dirdirmen and Dirdirwomen, lacking the
'noble divinity' and without 'secrets,' are thus held to
be deficient and somewhat clownish."

"Hmm," said Reith. "Why do you specify 'low-caste
Dirdirmen'? What of the Immaculates?"

Anacho cleared his throat. "The Immaculates obvi-
ate shame by elaborate surgical methods. They are allowed to alter themselves in accordance with one of
eight styles; thus they are conceded 'secrets' as well,
and may wear Blue and Pink."

"What about mating?"

"It is more difficult, and in fact becomes an inge-
nious analog of the Dirdir system. Each style will
match at most two styles of the other sex."

Reith could no longer restrain his mirth. Anacho listened with an expression half-grim, half-rueful. "What
of yourself?" asked Reith. "How far did you involve
yourself?"

"Not far enough," said Anacho. "For certain reasons I wore Blue and Pink without providing myself
the requisite 'secret.' I was declared an outlaw and an
atavism; this was my situation at our first meeting."

"A curious crime," said Reith.

Now Anacho darted for his life across the simulated
landscape of Sibol.

The avenue leading to the Glass Box became even
broader, as if in some attempt to keep it in scale with
the vast bulk. Those who walked the rasping white surface—Dirdir, Dirdirmen, common laborers in gray
cloaks—seemed artificial and unreal, like figures in
classical perspective exercises. As they walked they
looked neither right nor left, passing Reith and Traz as
if they were invisible.

Scarlet and purple spires reared to all sides; ahead
stood the Glass Box, dwarfing all else. Reith began to
suffer oppression of the spirit; Dirdir artifacts and the

human psyche were in discord. To tolerate such sur-
roundings, a man eventually must deny his heritage and
submit to the Dirdir world-view. In short, he must become a Dirdirman.

They came up beside two other men, like themselves
muffled in hooded gray cloaks. Reith spoke: "Perhaps
you will inform us. We want to visit the Glass Box but
we do not understand the procedure."

The two men gave him an uncertain appraisal. They
were father and son, both short, round-faced, with
round little paunches, thin arms and legs. The older
man said in a reedy voice, "One merely mounts by the
gray ramps; there is no more to know."

"You yourselves go to the Glass Box?"

"Yes. There is a special hunt at noon, for a great
Dirdirman villain, and there may well be a tossing."

"We had heard nothing of this. Who is this Dirdirman villain?"

The two again examined him dubiously, apparently
from a condition of innate uncertainty. "A renegade, a
blasphemer. We are scourers at the Number Four Fab-
rication Plant; we received information from the
Dirdirmen themselves."

"You go often to the Glass Box?"

"Often enough." The father spoke rather tersely.
The son amplified: "It is authorized and endorsed by
the Dirdirmen; there is no expense."

"Come," said the father. "We must hurry."

"If you have no objection," said Reith, "we will follow you and take advantage of your familiarity with
the procedures."

The father agreed with no great enthusiasm. "We do
not care to be delayed." The two set off up the avenue,
heads crouched upon their shoulders, a gait character-
istic to the Sivishe laborers. Imitating the sag-necked
slouch Reith and Traz followed. The glass walls reared
overhead like vitreous cliffs, showing spots of a red-
magenta glow where the illumination from within pene-
trated the glass. Angling along the sides were ramps
and escalators coded by color: purple, scarlet, mauve,

white and gray, each rising to different levels. The gray ramps led to a balcony only a hundred feet from the ground, evidently the lowest. Reith and Traz, joining a stream of men, women and children, climbed the ramp, passed through an ill-smelling passage which twisted forward and back and suddenly emerged upon a bright bleak expanse, illuminated by ten miniature suns. There were low crags and rolling hills, thickets of harsh vegetation: ocher, tan, yellow, bone-white, pale whitish brown. Below was a brackish pond, a thicket of hard white cactus-like growths; in the near distance stood a forest of bone-white spires identical in shape and size to the Dirdir residential towers. The similarity, thought Reith, could not be coincidental; on Sibol the Dirdir evidently inhabited hollow trees.

Somewhere among the hills and thickets wandered Anacho, in fear of his life, bitterly regretting the impulse which had brought him to Sivishe. But Anacho was not to be seen; in fact nowhere was there sign of either man or Dirdir. Reith turned to the two laborers for explanation.

"It is a quiet period," stated the father. "Notice the hill yonder? And its equal at the far north? These are base camps. During a quiet period the game takes refuge at one or the other of the camps. Let me see; where is my schedule?"

"I carry it," said the son. "Quiet continues yet an hour; the game is at this close hill."

"We are here in good time. According to rules of this particular cycle, there will be darkness in one hour, for a period of fourteen minutes. Then South Hill becomes fair territory and the game must vacate to North Hill, which in its turn becomes refuge. I am surprised that with so notorious a criminal, they do not allow Competition rules."

"The schedule was established last week," replied the son. "The criminal was taken only a day or so ago."

"We still may see good techniques, and perhaps a tossing or two."

"In one hour, then, the field goes dark?"

"For fourteen minutes, during which the hunt begins."

Reith and Traz returned to the outside balcony and the suddenly dim landscape of Tschai. Pulling their hoods close, hunching their necks, they sidled down the ramp to the ground.

Reith looked in all directions. Cloaked laborers marched stolidly up the gray ramp. Dirdirmen used the white ramps; Dirdir rode mauve, scarlet and purple escalators to the high balconies.

Reith went to the gray glass wall. He sat down and pretended to adjust his shoe. Traz stood in front of him. From his pouch Reith brought forth a pot of battarache and an attached timer. He carefully adjusted a dial, pulled a lever, laid it behind a shrub, against the glass wall.

No one heeded. He adjusted the timer on the second pot of battarache, gave pouch, battarache and timer to Traz. "You know what to do."

Traz reluctantly took the pouch. "The plan may succeed, but you and Anacho will both certainly be killed."

Reith pretended that Traz was wrong for once, for the encouragement of them both. "Drop off the battarache—you'll have to hurry. Remember, just opposite to here. There isn't much time. And I'll see you at the construction shed."

Traz turned away, concealing his face in the folds of his hood. "Very well, Adam Reith."

"But just in case something goes wrong: take the money and leave as fast as you can."

"Goodbye."

"Hurry now."

Reith watched the gray shape diminish along the base of the Glass Box. He drew a deep breath. There was little time. He must commit himself at once; if darkness arrived before he had located Anacho, all the effort and risk were in vain.

He returned back up the gray ramp, passed through the portal into the Sibol glare.

He scanned the field, taking careful note of landmarks and directions, then moved south around the deck, toward South Hill. The spectators became less numerous, most tending toward the middle or the north.

Reith selected a spot near a stanchion. He looked right and left. No one stood within two hundred feet of him. The decks above were empty. He brought out a coil of light rope, parted it, passed it around the stanchion, threw the parts down. With a look to right and left he swung himself over the rail, lowered himself to the hunting ground.

He did not go unnoticed. Pallid faces peered down in wonder. Reith paid them no heed. He no longer shared their world; he was game. He pulled the rope down and ran off toward South Hill, coiling the rope as he ran through forests of bristle, over limestone juts and coffee-colored chert.

He neared the first slopes of South Hill, sighting neither hunters nor game. The hunters would now be taking such positions as tactics dictated; the game would be lurking at the base of South Hill, wondering how best to reach the sanctuary of North Hill. Reith suddenly came upon a young Gray, crouched in the shadow of a white bamboo-like growth. He wore sandals and a breechclout; he carried a club and a cactus-prong dagger. Reith asked him, "Where is the Dirdirman, the one just put out on the field?"

The Gray gave his head an indifferent jerk. "There might be one such around the hill. Leave me; you create a flurry of darkness with your cloak. Drop it off; your skin is the best camouflage. Don't you know the Dirdir observe your every move?"

Reith ran on. He saw two elderly men, stark naked, with stringy muscles and white hair, standing poised like specters. Reith called out, "Have you seen a Dirdirman anywhere near?"

"Up beyond, or so it may be. Take yourself off, with your dark cloak."

Reith scrambled up a jut of sandstone. He called out: "Anacho!"

No response. Reith looked at his watch. In ten minutes the field would go dark. He searched the side of South Hill. A little distance away he glimpsed movement: persons running off through the thicket. His cloak seemed to arouse antagonism; he removed it, threw it over his arm.

In a hollow Reith found four men and a woman. They showed him the faces of hunted animals, and would not reply to his question. Reith labored up the hill, to gain a better view. "Anacho!" he called. A figure in a white smock swung around. Reith felt engulfed in relief; his knees felt weak; tears came to his eyes. "Anacho!"

"What do you do here!"

"Hurry. This way. We're about to escape."

Anacho looked at him in stupefaction. "No one escapes the Glass Box."

"Come along! You'll see!"

"Not that way," cried Anacho hoarsely. "Safety lies to the north, on North Hill! When the darkness comes the hunt starts!"

"I know, I know! We don't have much time. Come this way. We must take cover somewhere over yonder; we must be ready."

Anacho threw his hands in the air. "You must know something I don't know."

They ran back the way Reith had come, to the western face of South Hill. As they ran Reith gasped out the details of the plan.

Anacho asked in a hollow voice, "You did all this ... for me? You came down here on the field?"

"No matter about that. Now—we want to be close to that tall clump of white bristles. Where shall we take cover?"

"Within the clump—as good as any. Notice the hunters! They take their positions. They must keep off half a mile until the darkness comes. We are just barely within the sanctuary. Those four are marking us!"

"Darkness will be coming in seconds. Our plan is this: we run due west, toward that mound. From there we work to that bank of brown cactus and around the southern edge. Most important: we must not become separated!"

Anacho made a plaintive gesture. "How can we avoid it? We can't call out; the hunters will hear us."

Reith gave him an end of the rope. "Hold to that. And if we are separated we meet on the west edge of that yellow clump."

They waited for darkness. Out on the field the young Dirdir took up their positions, with here and there more experienced hunters. Reith looked to the east. By some trick of light and atmosphere the field seemed to be open and to extend to far horizons; only by dint of concentration could Reith make out the east wall.

Darkness came. The lights dulled to red, flickered out. Far to the north glowed a single purple light, to indicate direction. It cast no illumination. Darkness was complete. The hunt had begun. From the north came Dirdir hunting calls: chilling hoots and ululations.

Reith and Anacho moved west. From time to time they halted to listen through the dark. To their right came a sinister jingling. They stood stock-still. The jingling and a *pad-pad-pad* faded off to the rear.

They arrived at their landmark hummock, and continued toward the clump of cactus. Something was near. They halted to listen. It seemed to their straining ears, or nerves, that something else paused as well.

From high, high above came a many-voiced cry, ranging up and down the sonic range, then another and another. "The hunt-calls of all the septs," Anacho whispered. "A traditional ritual. Now from the field, all the sept-members present must give voice." The calls from above halted; from all parts of the hunting field, eerie out of the dark, came the responses. Anacho nudged Reith. "While the responses sound, we are free to move. Come."

They set out with long strides, their feet sensitive as eyes. The hunt-slogans dwindled away into the distance; again there was silence. Reith struck a loose rock with his feet, to cause a distressing rattle. They froze, teeth gritted.

There was no reaction. On they walked, on and on, feeling out with their feet for the cactus clump, but encountering only air and harsh soil. Reith began to fear that they had passed it by, that the lights would go on to expose them to all the hunters, all the spectators.

Seven minutes of darkness had elapsed, or so he estimated. In another minute, at the latest, they should find the outskirts of the clump. . . . A sound! Running feet, apparently human, passed not thirty feet distant. A moment later a jogging thud, shrill whispers, a jingle of hunting gear. The sounds passed, dwindled. Silence returned.

Seconds later they came to the cactus. "Around to the southern side," Reith whispered. "Then on hands and knees into the center."

The two pushed through the coarse stalks, meeting sharp side-prongs.

"Light! Here it comes!"

The dark began to dissipate in the style of a Sibol sunrise: up through gray, pallid white, into the full glare of day.

Reith and Anacho looked about them. The cactus provided fair concealment; they seemed in no imminent peril, though not a hundred yards distant three Dirdir scions bounded across the field, heads high, searching in all directions for fleeing game. Reith consulted his watch. Fifteen minutes remained—if Traz had suffered no mishap, if he had been able to reach the opposite wall of the Glass Box.

The forest of white bristle lay a quarter of a mile ahead, across somewhat open ground. It might, thought Reith, be the longest quarter-mile he had ever traversed.

The two wormed through the cactus to the northern verge. "The hunters keep to middle ground for an hour or so," said Anacho. "They restrain quick penetration to the north, then they work to the south."

Reith handed Anacho a power-gun, tucked his own into his waistband. He raised to his knees. A mile distant he glimpsed movement, Dirdir or game he could not be sure. Anacho suddenly pulled him down into concealment. From behind the cactus bush trotted a group of Immaculates, hands sheathed in artificial talons, simulated effulgences trailing over their shining white pates. Reith's stomach twisted; he stifled the impulse to confront the creatures, to shoot them.

The Dirdirmen loped past, and it seemed that they missed seeing the fugitives only through the sheerest chance. They angled away to the east, and, sighting game, bounded off at full speed.

Reith checked his watch; time was growing short. Rising to his knees, he looked in all directions. "Let's go."

They jumped erect, ran off for the white forest.

They paused halfway, crouched behind a little thicket. By South Hill a hot hunt was in progress; two bands of hunters converged on game which had taken cover on South Hill itself. Reith checked his watch. Nine minutes. The white forest was only a minute or two away. The lone spire which he had established as a landmark could now be seen, a few hundred yards west of the forest. They set forth again. Four hunters stepped from the forest, where they had stationed themselves to spy out the game. Reith's heart sank into his boots. "Keep going," he said to Anacho. "We'll fight them."

Anacho looked dubiously at the power-gun. "If they take us with guns, they'll toss us for days . . . but I was to be tossed in any event."

The Dirdir watched in fascination as Reith and Anacho approached. "We must take them into the forest," muttered Anacho. "The judges will intervene if they see our guns."

"Around to the left then, and behind that clump of yellow grass."

The Dirdir did not advance to meet them, but moved to the side. With a final burst Reith and Anacho gained the edge of the forest. The Dirdir screamed their hunt slogan and sprang forward, while Reith and Anacho retreated.

"Now," said Reith. They brought forth their guns. The Dirdir gave a croak of dismay. Four quick shots: four dead Dirdir. Instantly from high above came a great howl: a mind-jarring ululation. Anacho shouted out in sheer frustration, "The judges saw. They'll watch us now, and direct the hunt. We are lost."

"We have a chance," Reith insisted. He wiped the sweat from his face, squinting against the glare. "In three minutes—if all goes well—the explosion. Let's go on to the long spire."

They ran through the forest, and as they emerged they saw hunt-teams loping in their direction. The howling overhead rose and fell, then stopped.

They reached the single spire, with the glass wall only a hundred yards distant. Above, obscured by glare and reflections, ran the observation decks; Reith was barely able to make out the gaping spectators.

He checked his watch.

Now.

An interval, to be expected: the Box was three miles across. Seconds passed, then came a great puff of shock and a thunderous reverberation. Lights flickered; far to the east they were extinguished. Reith peered but could not see the effect of the blast. From overhead, up and down the length of the field, came a frantic baying, expressing rage so savage and stupendous that Reith's knees became weak.

Anacho was more matter-of-fact. "They direct all hunts east to the rupture, to prevent the escape of game."

The hunts which had been converging upon Reith and Anacho turned and raced off to the east.

"Get ready," said Reith. He looked at his watch. "To the ground."

A second explosion: a tremendous shatter to gladden Reith's heart, to lift him into a state of near religious exaltation. Shards and chunks of gray glass whistled overhead; the lights dimmed, went dark. Before them appeared a gap, like an opening into a new dimension, a hundred feet wide, almost as high as the first observation deck.

Reith and Anacho jumped to their feet. Without difficulty they reached the wall and sprang through— away from the arid Sibol, out into the dim Tschai afternoon.

Down the broad white avenue they ran, then at Anacho's direction turned off to the north, toward the factories and the white Dirdirman spires, then to the waterfront, and across the causeway into Sivishe.

They halted to catch their breath. "Best that you go direct to the sky-car," said Reith. "Take it and leave. You won't be safe in Sivishe."

"Woudiver issued the information against me; he'll do the same for you," said Anacho.

"I can't leave Sivishe now, with the spaceship so near to completion. Woudiver and I must have an understanding."

"Never," said Anacho bleakly. "He is a great wad of malice."

"He can't betray the spaceship without endangering himself," argued Reith. "He is our accomplice; we work in his shed."

"He'd explain it away somehow."

"Perhaps, perhaps not. In any event, you must leave Sivishe. We'll share the money—then you must go. The sky-car is no more use to me."

Anacho's white face became mulish. "Not so fast. I am not the goal of a *tsau'gsh*, remember this. Who will take the initiative to seek me out?"

Reith looked back toward the Glass Cage. "You don't think they'll seek you in Sivishe?"

"They are unpredictable. But I'm as safe in Sivishe

as anywhere else. I can't go back to the Ancient Realm. They won't seek me at the shed unless Woudiver betrays the project."

"Woudiver must be controlled," said Reith.

Anacho only grunted. They set off once more, through the mean alleys of Sivishe.

The sun passed behind the spires of Hei and dimness seeped into the already shadowed streets. Reith and Anacho rode by public power-wagon to the shed. Woudiver's office was dark; within the shed dim lights glimmered. The mechanics had gone home; there seemed to be no one on the premises. . . . In the shadows a figure moved. "Traz!" cried Reith.

The lad came forward. "I knew that you would come here, if you won free."

Neither the nomads nor the Dirdirmen were given to demonstration; Anacho and Traz merely took note of each other.

"Best that we leave this place," said Traz. "And quickly."

"I said to Anacho, I say to you: take the sky-car and go. There is no reason for you to risk another day in Sivishe."

"And what about you?"

"I must take my chances here."

"The chances are very small, what with Woudiver and his vindictiveness."

"I will control Woudiver."

"An impossibility!" Anacho cried out. "Who can control such perversity, so much monstrous passion? He is beyond reason."

Reith nodded somberly. "There is only one certain way, and it may be difficult."

"How do you intend this miracle?" Anacho demanded.

"I intend simply to take him at gunpoint, and bring him here. If he will not come, I will kill him. If he comes, he will be my captive, under constant guard. I can think of nothing better."

Anacho grunted. "I would not object to guarding Big Yellow."

"The time to act is now," said Traz. "Before he knows of the escape."

"For you two, no!" Reith declared. "If I get killed . . . too bad but unavoidable. It is a risk I have to take. Not so for you. Take the sky-car and money, leave now while you are able!"

"I remain," said Traz.

"And I as well," said Anacho.

Reith made a gesture of defeat. "Let's go after Woudiver."

Chapter 18

The three stood in the dark court outside Woudiver's apartments, judging how best to open the postern. "We don't dare force the lock," muttered Anacho. "Woudiver undoubtedly guards himself with alarms and deathtraps."

"We'll have to go over the top," said Reith. "It shouldn't be too hard to reach the roof." He studied the wall, the cracked tile, a twisted old psilla. "Nothing to it." He pointed. "Up there—across to there—then there and over."

Anacho shook his head gloomily. "I'm surprised to find you still so innocent. Why do you think the route appears so simple? Because Woudiver is convinced no one can climb? Bah. You'd find stings, traps and jangle-buttons every place you put your hand."

Reith chewed his lip in mortification. "Well, then, how do you propose we get in?"

"Not through here," said Anacho. "We must defeat Woudiver's craft with cleverness of our own."

Traz made a sudden motion, and drew the other two back into the deep shadows of an area-way.

Along the alley came a shuffle of footsteps. A tall thin shape limped past them and went to stand by the postern. Traz whispered: "Deine Zarre! He's in a bitter state."

Deine Zarre stood motionless; he brought forth a tool and worked on the lock. The postern swung open; he walked through, his pace inexorable as doom. Reith sprang forward and held the gate ajar. Deine Zarre limped on unseeing. Traz and Anacho passed through the postern; Reith let the gate rest against the lock. They now stood in a paved loggia, with a dimly lit passage leading to the main bulk of the house. "For the moment," said Reith, "you two wait here; let me confront Woudiver alone."

"You'll be in great danger," said Anacho. "It's obvious that you came for no good!"

"Not necessarily!" said Reith. "He will be suspicious, certainly. But he can't know that I've seen you. If he sees the three of us he'll be on his guard. Alone, I have a better chance of outwitting him."

"Very well," said Anacho. "We'll wait here, for a certain period, at any rate. Then we'll come in after you."

"Give me fifteen minutes." Reith set off down the passage, which opened into a courtyard. Across, in front of a brass-bound door, stood Deine Zarre, plying his tool. Light suddenly flooded the courtyard. Deine Zarre had apparently tripped an alarm.

Into the courtyard stepped Artilo. "Zarre," he said.

Deine Zarre turned about.

"What do you do here?" Artilo asked in a gentle voice.

"It is no concern of yours," said Deine Zarre tonelessly. "Leave me be."

With an uncharacteristic flourish, Artilo brought forth a power-gun. "I have been so ordered. Prepare to die."

Reith stepped quickly forward, but the motion of Deine Zarre's eyes gave warning to Artilo; he started to look about. With two long strides, Reith was on him.

He struck a terrible blow at the base of Artilo's skull, and Artilo collapsed dead. Reith took up the power-gun, rolled Artilo to the side. Deine Zarre was already turning away, as if the circumstances held no interest.

Reith said, "Wait!"

Deine Zarre turned around once more. Reith came forward. Deine Zarre's gray eyes were astonishingly clear. Reith asked, "Why are you here?"

"To kill Woudiver. He has savaged my children." Deine Zarre's voice was calm and expository. "They are dead, both dead, and gone from this sad world Tschai."

Reith's voice sounded muffled and distant to his own ears. "Woudiver must be destroyed . . . but not until the ship is complete."

"He will never let you complete the ship."

"That is why I am here."

"What can you do?" Deine Zarre spoke contemptuously.

"I intend to take him captive, and keep him until the ship is finished. Then you may kill him."

"Very well," said Deine Zarre in a dull voice. "Why not? I will make him suffer."

"As you please. You go ahead. I will come close behind, as before. When we find Woudiver, upbraid him, but offer no violence. We don't want to drive him to desperate action."

Deine Zarre turned without a word. He worked open the door, to reveal a room furnished in scarlet and yellow. Deine Zarre entered, and after a quick look over his shoulder Reith followed. A dwarfish, dark-skinned servant in an enormous white turban stood startled.

"Where is Aila Woudiver?" asked Deine Zarre in his most gentle voice.

The servant became haughty. "He is importantly busy. He has great dealings. He cannot be disturbed."

Seizing the servant by the scruff of the neck Reith half raised him off the ground, dislodging the turban. The servant keened in pain and wounded dignity.

"What are you doing? Take your hands away or I will summon my master!"

"Precisely what we want you to do," said Reith.

The servant stood back, rubbing his neck and glaring at Reith. "Leave the house at once!"

"Take us to Woudiver, if you want to avoid trouble!"

The servant began to whine. "I may not do so. He'll have me whipped!"

"Look yonder in the courtyard," said Deine Zarre. "You'll see Artilo's dead body. Do you wish to join him?"

The servant began to shake and fell on his knees. Reith hoisted him erect. "Quick now! To Woudiver!"

"You must tell him I was forced, on threat of my life!" cried the servant with chattering teeth. "Then you must swear—"

The portiere at the far end of the room parted. The great face of Aila Woudiver peered through. "What is this disturbance?"

Reith pushed the servant away. "Your man refused to summon you."

Woudiver examined him with the cleverest and most suspicious gaze imaginable. "For good reason. I am occupied with important affairs."

"None so important as mine," said Reith.

"A moment," said Woudiver. He turned, spoke a word or two to his visitors, swaggered back into the scarlet and yellow salon. "You have the money?"

"Yes, of course. Would I be here otherwise?"

For another long moment Woudiver surveyed Reith. "Where is the money?"

"In a safe place."

Woudiver chewed at his pendulous lower lip. "Do not use that tone with me. To be candid, I suspect you of contriving an infamy, that which today allowed the escape of numerous criminals from the Glass Box."

Reith chuckled. "Tell me, if you please, how I could be two places at once?"

"If you were in a single place, that is enough to

damn you. A man corresponding to your description lowered himself to the field only an hour before the event. He would not have done so had he not been sure of escape. It is noteworthy that the renegade Dirdirman seemed to be among those missing."

Deine Zarre spoke: "The battarache came from your store; you will be held responsible if I should utter a word."

Woudiver seemed to notice Deine Zarre for the first time. In simulated surprise he spoke. "What do you do here, old man? Better be off about your business."

"I came to kill you," said Deine Zarre. "Reith asked that I wait."

"Come along, Woudiver," said Reith. "The game is over." He displayed his weapon. "Quickly, or I'll burn some of your hide."

Woudiver looked from one to the other without apparent concern. "Do the mice bare their teeth?"

Reith, from long experience, knew enough to expect wrangling, obstinacy, and generally perverse behavior. In a resigned voice he said, "Come along, Woudiver."

Woudiver smiled. "Two ridiculous little submen." He raised his voice a trifle. "Artilo!"

"Artilo is dead," said Deine Zarre. He looked right and left in something like puzzlement. Woudiver watched him blandly. "You seek something?"

Deine Zarre, ignoring Woudiver, muttered to Reith, "He is too easy, even for Woudiver. Take care."

Reith said in a sharp voice, "On the count of five, I'll burn you."

"First, a question," said Woudiver. "Where do we go?"

Reith ignored him. "One . . . two . . ."

Woudiver sighed hugely. "You fail to amuse me."

". . . three . . ."

"Somehow I must protect myself. . . ."

". . . four . . ."

". . . so much is clear." Woudiver backed against the wall. The velvet canopy instantly slumped upon Reith and Deine Zarre.

Reith fired the gun but the folds struck down his arm, and the ray scarred only the black and white tiles of the floor.

Woudiver's chuckle sounded muffled but rich and unctuous. The floor vibrated to his ominous tread. A vast weight suffocated Reith; Woudiver had flung himself down upon his body. Reith lay half-dazed. Woudiver's voice sounded close. "So the jackanapes thought to trouble Aila Woudiver? See how he is now!" The weight lifted. "And Deine Zarre, who courteously refrained from assassination. Well then, farewell, Deine Zarre. I am more decisive."

A sound, a sad sodden gurgle and then a scraping of fingernails upon the tiles.

"Adam Reith," said the voice. "You are a peculiar mad case. I am interested in your intentions. Drop the gun, put your arms to the front and do not move. Do you feel the weight on your neck? That is my foot. Quick then, arms forward, and no sudden motions. Hisziu, make ready."

The folds were pulled back, away from Reith's extended arms. Nimble dark fingers bound his wrists with silk ribbon.

The velvet was further drawn back. Reith, still somewhat dazed, looked up at the spraddle-legged bulk. Hisziu the servant skipped back and forth, around and under, like a puppy.

Woudiver hoisted Reith erect. "Walk, if you will." He sent Reith stumbling with a shove.

Chapter 19

In a dark room, against a metal rack, stood Reith. His outstretched arms were taped to a transverse bar; his ankles were likewise secured. No light entered

the room save the glimmer of a few stars through a
narrow window. Hisziu the servant crouched four feet
in front of him, with a light whip of braided silk, little
more than a length of supple cord attached to a short
handle. He seemed able to see in the dark and amused
himself by snapping the tip of the whip, at unpredictable intervals, upon Reith's wrists, knees and chin. He
spoke only once. "Your two friends have been taken.
They are no better than you: worse, indeed. Woudiver
works with them."

Reith stood limp, his thoughts sluggish and dismal.
Disaster was complete; he was conscious of nothing
else. The malicious little snaps of Hisziu's whip barely
brushed the edge of his awareness. His existence was
coming to an end, to be no more remarked than the
fall of a raindrop into one of Tschai's sullen oceans.
Somewhere out of sight the blue moon rose, casting a
sheen across the sky. The slow waxing and equally
slow waning of moonlight told the passing of the night.

Hisziu fell into a drowse and snored softly. Reith
was indifferent. He raised his head, looked out the window. The shimmer of moonlight was gone; a muddy
color toward the east signaled the coming of Carina
4269. Hisziu awoke with a start, and flicked the whip
petulantly at Reith's cheeks, raising instant blood-
blisters. He left the chamber and a moment later returned with a mug of hot tea, which he sipped by the
window. Reith croaked: "I'll pay you ten thousand sequins to cut me loose."

Hisziu paid him no heed.

Reith said, "And another ten thousand if you help
me free my friends."

The servant sipped the tea as if Reith had never
spoken.

The sky glowed dark gold; Carina 4269 had appeared. Steps sounded; Woudiver's bulk filled the doorway. A moment he stood quietly, assessing the
situation, then, seizing the whip, he gestured Hisziu
from the room.

Woudiver seemed exalted, as if drugged or drunk.

He slapped the whip against his thigh. "I can't find the money, Adam Reith. Where is it?"

Reith attempted to speak in a casual voice. "What are your plans?"

Woudiver raised his hairless eyebrows. "I have no plans. Events proceed; I exist as well as I may."

"Why do you keep me tied here?"

Aila Woudiver slapped the whip against his leg. "I have naturally notified my kinsmen of your apprehension."

"The Dirdir?"

"Of course." Woudiver gave his thigh a rap with the whip.

Reith spoke with great earnestness. "The Dirdir are no kinsmen of yours! Dirdir and men are not even remotely connected; they come from different stars."

Woudiver leaned indolently against the wall. "Where do you learn such idiocy?"

Reith licked his lips, wondering where lay his best hope of succor. Woudiver was not a rational man; he was motivated by instinct and intuition. Reith tried to project utter certainty as he spoke. "Men originated on the planet Earth. The Dirdir know this as well as I. They prefer that Dirdirmen deceive themselves."

Woudiver nodded thoughtfully. "You intend to seek out this 'Earth' with your spaceship?"

"I don't need to seek it out. It lies two hundred lightyears distant, in the constellation Clari."

Woudiver pranced forward. With his yellow face a foot from Reith's he bellowed, "And what of the treasure you promised me? You misled, you deceived!"

"No," said Reith. "I did not. I am an Earthman. I was shipwrecked here on Tschai. Help me back to Earth; you will receive whatever treasure you care to name."

Woudiver backed slowly away. "You are one of the Yao redemptionist cult, whatever it calls itself."

"No. I am telling the truth. Your best interest lies in helping me."

Woudiver nodded sagely. "Perhaps this is the case.

But first things first. You can easily demonstrate your good faith. Where is my money?"

"*Your* money? It is not your money. It is my money."

"A sterile distinction. Where is, shall we say, *our* money?"

"You'll never see it unless you perform your obligations."

"This is utter obstinacy!" stormed Woudiver. "You are captured, you are done, and your henchmen as well. The Dirdirman must return to the Glass Cage. The steppe-boy will be sold into slavery—unless you care to buy his life with the money."

Reith sagged and became listless. Woudiver strutted back and forth across the room, darting glances at Reith. He came close and prodded Reith in the stomach with the whip. "Where is the money?"

"I don't trust you," said Reith in a dreary voice. "You never keep your promises." With a great effort, he lifted himself erect and tried to speak in a calm voice. "If you want the money, let me go free. The spaceship is almost finished. You may come along to Earth."

Woudiver's face was inscrutable. "And then?"

"A space-yacht, a palace—whatever you want. You shall have it."

"And how shall I return to Sivishe?" demanded Woudiver scornfully. "What of my affairs? It is plain that you are mad; why do I waste my time? Where is the money? The Dirdirman and the steppe-lad have declared with conviction that they do not know."

"I don't know either. I gave it to Deine Zarre and told him to hide it. You killed him."

Woudiver stifled a groan of dismay. "My money?"

"Tell me," said Reith, "do you intend that I finish the spaceship?"

"It has never been my intention!"

"You defrauded me?"

"Why not? You tried the same. The man that beats Aila Woudiver is cunning indeed."

"No question as to that."

Hisziu entered the room and, standing on tiptoe, whispered into Woudiver's ear. Woudiver stamped with rage. "So soon? They are early! I have not even started." He turned to Reith, his face seething like water in a boiling pot. "Quick then, the money, or I sell the lad. Quick!"

"Let us go! Help us finish the spaceship. Then you shall have your money!"

"You unreasonable ingrate!" hissed Woudiver. Footsteps sounded. "I am thwarted!" he groaned. "What a sad life is mine. Vermin!" Woudiver spat into Reith's face and beat him furiously with the whip.

Into the room, proudly conducted by Hisziu, came a tall Dirdirman, the most splendid and strange Reith had yet seen: by all odds an Immaculate. Woudiver muttered to Hisziu from the side of his mouth; Reith's bonds were cut. The Dirdirman attached a chain to Reith's neck, clasped the other end to his belt. Without a word he walked away, shaking his fingers in fastidious disdain.

Reith stumbled after.

Chapter 20

Before Woudiver's house stood a white-enameled car. The Immaculate snapped Reith's chain to a ring at the rear. Reith watched him in dreary wonder. The Immaculate stood almost seven feet tall, with artificial effulgences attached to wens at either side of his peaked scalp. His skin gleamed white as the enamel of the car; his head was totally hairless; his nose was a ridged beak. For all his strange appearance and undoubtedly altered sexuality, he was a man, ruminated Reith, derived from the same soil as himself. From the house,

at a quick stumble, as if shoved, came Anacho and
Traz. Chains encircled their necks; behind, jerking the
loose ends, ran Hisziu. Two Dirdirman Elites followed.
They shackled the chains to the back of the car. The
Immaculate spoke a few sibilant words to Anacho and
indicated a shelf running across the rear of the car.
Without looking back, he stepped into the car, where
the two Elites already sat. Anacho muttered, "Climb
aboard, otherwise we'll be dragged."

The three crawled up on the rear shelf, clutched the
rings to which their neck chains were shackled. In such
undignified fashion they departed Woudiver's residence. Woudiver's black saloon trundled fifty yards behind, with Woudiver's huge bulk crouched over the
steering apparatus.

"He wants recognition," said Anacho. "He has assist-
ed at an important hunt; he wants a share of the
status."

"I made the mistake," said Reith in a thick voice,
"of dealing with Woudiver as if he were a man. If I
had treated him as an animal we might be better off."

"We could hardly be worse."

"Where are we going?"

"To the Glass Box; where else?"

"We are to have no hearing, no opportunity to speak
for ourselves?"

"Naturally not," said Anacho curtly. "You are submen. I am a renegade."

The white car veered into a plaza and halted. The
Dirdirmen alighted and stood stiffly apart, watching the
sky. A plump middle-aged man in a rich dark brown
suit came forward: a person of status and evident van-
ity, with his hair elaborately curled and jeweled. He
addressed the Dirdirmen in an easy manner; they replied after a moment's meaningful silence.

"That is Erlius, Administrator of Sivishe," grunted
Anacho. "He wants to be in at the kill too. It seems
that we are important game."

Attracted by the activity, the folk of Sivishe began to
gather around the white car. They formed a wide re-

spectful circle, eyeing the captives with macabre speculation, crouching back whenever the glance of a
Dirdirman drifted in their direction.

Woudiver remained in his car, at a distance of fifty
yards or so, apparently arranging his thoughts. At last
he alighted and seemed to concern himself with the
matter indited on a fold of paper. Erlius, noticing,
quickly turned his back.

"Look at the two of them," growled Anacho. "Each
hates the other: Woudiver ridicules Erlius for lacking
Dirdirman blood; Erlius would like to see Woudiver in
the Glass Box."

"So would I," said Reith. "Speaking of the Glass
Box, why are we waiting?"

"For the leaders of the *tsau'gsh*. You will see the
Glass Box soon enough."

Reith fretfully wrenched at the chain. The Dirdirmen turned him glances of admonition. "Ridiculous,"
muttered Reith. "There must be something we can do.
What of the Dirdir traditions? What if I cried *h'sai
h'sai, h'sai,* or whatever the call for arbitration?"

"The call is *dr'ssa dr'ssa, dr'ssa!*"

"What would happen if I called for arbitration?'

"You would be no better than before. The arbitrator
would find you guilty and, as before: the Glass Box."

"And if I challenged the arbitration?"

"You'd be forced to fight, and killed all the sooner."

"And no one can be taken unless he is accused?"

"In theory," said Anacho curtly, "that is the custom.
Who do you plan to challenge? Woudiver? It will do
no good. He has not accused you, but only cooperated
with the hunt."

"We will see."

Traz pointed into the sky. "Here come the Dirdir."

Anacho studied the descending sky-car. "The Thisz
crest. If the Thisz are involved, we can expect brisk
treatment indeed. They may even issue a proscription,
that none but Thisz can hunt us."

Traz strained against the chain shackle without
avail. He gave a hiss of frustration and turned to watch

the descending sky-car. The gray-hooded crowd drew
back from underneath; the sky-car landed not fifty feet
from the white vehicle. Five Dirdir alighted: an Excellent and four of lower caste.

The Immaculate Dirdirman stepped grandly forward, but the Dirdir ignored him with the same indifference he had shown Erlius.

For a moment or two the Dirdir appraised Reith,
Anacho and Traz. Then they made a signal to the Immaculate and uttered a few brief sounds.

Erlius stepped forward to pay his respects, knees
bent, head bobbing. Before he could speak Woudiver
marched forward and thrust his vast yellow bulk in
front of Erlius, who was forced to stumble aside.

Woudiver spoke in a high-pitched voice: "Here,
Thisz dignitaries, are the criminals sought by the hunt.
I have participated to no small degree; let this be noted
upon my scroll of honors!"

The Dirdir gave him only cursory attention.
Woudiver, apparently expecting no more, bowed his
head, swung his arms in an elaborate flourish.

The Immaculate approached the captives and un-
snapped the chains. Reith snatched his chain free. The
Immaculate looked up in slack-jawed surprise, the false
effulgences drooping to the side of his white face. Reith
walked forward, heart pounding in his throat. He felt
the pressure of every eye; with great effort he held his
gait to a steady, deliberate step. Six feet in front of the
Dirdir he halted, so close that he could smell their
body odor. They regarded him without display of any
kind.

Reith raised his voice in order to speak clearly:
"Dr'ssa! Dr'ssa! Dr'ssa!"

The Dirdir made small movements of surprise.

"Dr'ssa! Dr'ssa! Dr'ssa!" Reith called once more.

The Excellent spoke in a nasal, oboe-sounding voice.
"Why do you cry *dr'ssa?* You are a subman, incapable
of discrimination."

"I am a man, your superior. Hence I cry *dr'ssa.*"

Woudiver pushed forward with a self-important huffing and heaving. "Bah! He is mad!"

The Dirdir seemed somewhat perplexed. Reith called out, "Who accuses me? Of what crime? Let him come forward and let the case be judged by an arbitrator."

The Excellent spoke: "You invoke a traditional force stronger than contempt or disgust. You may not be denied. Who accuses this submas?"

Woudiver spoke. "I accuse Adam Reith of blasphemy, of disputing the Doctrine of Double Genesis, of claiming status equal to the Dirdir. He has stated that Dirdirmen are not the pure line of the Second Yolk; he has called them a race of mutated freaks. He insists that men derive from a planet other than Sibol. This is not in accord with orthodox doctrine, and is repugnant. He is a mischief-maker, a liar, a provocator." Woudiver accented each of his accusations with a stab of his massive forefinger. "Such are my charges!" He favored the Dirdir with a companionable smirk, then turned and roared at the crowd, "Stand back! Do not press so close upon the dignitaries!"

The Dirdir fluted to Reith, "You claim this accusation to be false?"

Reith stood in perplexity. He faced a dilemma. To deny the charge was to endorse Dirdirman orthodoxy. He asked cautiously, "Essentially, I am accused of unorthodox views. Is this a crime?"

"Certainly, if the arbitrator declares it so."

"What if these views are accurate?"

"Then you must hold the arbitrator to account. Ridiculous as such an eventuality may be, it is tradition and wields its own force."

"Who is the arbitrator?"

The polished bone countenance of the Excellent showed no change, nor did his voice. "In this instance I appoint the Immaculate yonder."

The Immaculate stepped forward. In plangent mock-Dirdir tones he spoke: "I will be expeditious; the ordinary ceremonies are inappropriate." He spoke to Reith. "Do you deny the charges?"

"I neither confirm nor deny them; they are ridiculous."

"It is my opinion that your statement is evasive. It signifies guilt. Additionally your attitudes are disrespectful. You are guilty."

"I refuse to accept your verdict," said Reith, "unless you can enforce it. I hold you to account."

The Immaculate regarded Reith with scorn and revulsion. "You challenge me, an Immaculate?"

"It seems to be the only way I can prove my innocence."

The Immaculate looked at the Dirdir Excellent. "Am I so obligated?"

"You are so obligated."

The Immaculate measured Reith. "I will kill you with my hands and teeth as befits a Dirdirman."

"As you please. First, remove this chain from my neck."

"Remove the chain," said the Dirdir Excellent.

The Immaculate said fretfully, "Vulgarity! I lose dignity performing before a gaggle of submen."

"Do not complain," said the Excellent. "It is I, Captain of the Hunt, who loses a trophy. Continue; enforce your arbitration."

The chain was removed. Reith stretched, relaxed, stretched, relaxed, hoping to restore tone to his muscles. He had hung all night by his wrists; his body felt heavy with fatigue. The Dirdirman stepped forward. Reith became a trifle light-headed.

"What are the rules of combat?" asked Reith. "I do not wish to commit any fouls upon you."

"There are no fouls," said the Immaculate. "We use hunt rules: you are my game!" He uttered a wild screech and launched himself upon Reith, in what seemed an ineffectual sprawl, until Reith touched the creature's white body and found it all tense muscle and gristle. Reith fended aside the rush, but was ripped by artificial talons. He attempted an armlock, but could not secure a leverage. He struck the Immaculate a blow under the ear, tried to hack the larynx and missed. The Immaculate stood back in annoyance. The spectators gasped in excitement. The Immaculate again launched himself upon Reith, who caught the long forearm and sent the Dirdirman staggering. Woudiver could not contain himself; he rushed out and struck Reith a buffet across the side of his head. Traz yelled in protest and whipped his chain across Woudiver's face. Woudiver screamed in agony and sat squashily upon the ground. Anacho wrapped his chain around Woudiver's neck and yanked it tight. The Elite Dirdirman leaped forward, snatched away the chain. Woudiver lay gasping, his face the color of mud.

The Immaculate had taken advantage of Woudiver's attack to seize Reith and bear him to the ground. The wire-tense arms clasped Reith's body; sharp long teeth tore at his neck. Reith freed his arms. With all his force he clapped his cupped hands upon the white ears. The Immaculate emitted a strangled squeal and rolled his head in agony. Momentarily he went limp. Reith straddled the thin body, as if he rode a white eel. He began to work at the bald head. He tore away the false effulgences, teased the head this way and that, then gave a great twist. The Immaculate's head hung askew; his body thrashed and floundered, then lay still.

Reith rose to his feet. He stood shaking and panting. "I am vindicated," he said.

"The charges of the fat subman are invalid," intoned the Excellent. "He may therefore be held to account."

Reith turned away. "Halt!" said the Excellent, its voice taking on a throaty vibrato. "Are there further charges?"

A Dirdir of the Elite caste, effulgences rigid and sparkling with crystal coruscations, spoke: "Does the beast still call dr'ssa?"

Reith swung around, half-intoxicated by fatigue and the aftermath of struggle. "I am a man; you are the beast."

"Do you demand arbitration?" the Excellent asked. "If not, let us be away."

Reith's heart sank. "What are the new charges?"

The Elite stepped forward. "I charge that you and your henchmen trespassed upon the Dirdir Hunting Preserve and there treacherously slaughtered members of the Thisz Sept."

"I deny the charge," said Reith in a hoarse voice.

The Elite turned to the Excellent. "I request that you arbitrate. I request that you give me this beast and his henchmen and mark him exclusive quarry of the Thisz."

"I accept the onus of arbitration," fluted the Excellent. To Reith, in a tone nasal and coarse: "You trespassed in the Carabas, this is true."

"I entered the Carabas. No one ordered me not to do so."

"The proscription is general knowledge. You furtively assaulted several Dirdir; this is true."

"I assaulted no one who did not attack me first. If the Dirdir wish to act like wild beasts then they must suffer the consequences."

From the crowd came a murmur of wonder and what seemed muted approval. The Excellent turned to glance around the plaza. Instantly the sound was muted.

"It is Dirdir tradition to hunt. It is subman tradition and his essential character to serve as quarry."

"I am no subman," said Reith. "I am a man and quarry to no one. If a wild beast attacks me I will kill it."

The bone-white face of the Excellent showed no quiver of feeling. But the effulgences began to glow, and to become rigid. "The verdict must adhere to tradition," the creature intoned. "I find against the subman. This farrago is now at an end. You must be taken to the Glass Cage."

"I challenge the arbitration!" cried Reith. Stepping forward, he buffeted the Excellent on the side of the head. The skin was cold and somewhat flexible, like tortoiseshell; Reith's hand stung from the blow. The Excellent's effulgences stood like hot wires; it vented a thin whistle. The crowd stood in unbelieving silence.

The Excellent reached its great arms to the front in a clutching, rippling gesture. It vented a gurgling scream and poised to leap.

"A moment," said Reith, stepping back. "What are the rules of combat?"

"There are no rules. I kill as I choose."

"And if I kill you, I am vindicated, and my friends as well?"

"That is the case."

"Let us fight with swords."

"We will fight as we stand."

"Very well," said Reith.

The fight was no contest. The Excellent came forward, swift and massive as a tiger. Reith took two quick steps back; the Excellent launched itself. Reith seized the horny wrist, planted a foot in the torso; falling backward he threw the creature in a sprawling somersault. It landed on its neck, to lay in a daze. Instantly Reith was upon it, locking the taloned arms. The Excellent writhed and thrashed; Reith banged its head against the pavement until the bone cracked and whitish-green ichor began to exude. He panted: "What of the arbitration? Was it right or wrong?"

The Excellent keened—a weird wailing sound, expressing no emotion known to human experience. Reith banged down the harsh white head again and again. "What of the arbitration?" He slammed the head against the pavement. The Dirdir made a great effort to dislodge Reith and failed. "You are the victor. My arbitration is refuted."

"And I, with my friends, are now held guiltless? We may pursue our activities without persecution?"

"This is the case."

Reith called to Anacho, "Can I trust it?"

Anacho said, "Yes, it is tradition. If you want a trophy, pluck out his effulgences."

"I want no trophy." Reith rose to his feet and stood swaying.

The crowd regarded him with awe. Erlius turned on his heel and strode hastily away. Aila Woudiver backed slowly toward his black car.

Reith pointed a finger: "Woudiver—your charges were false and you now must answer to me."

Woudiver snatched out his power-gun; Traz leaped forward, hung on the vast wrist. The gun discharged, scorching Woudiver's leg. He bawled in agony and fell to the ground. Anacho took the gun; Reith tied one of the chains around Woudiver's neck and gave it a harsh tug. "Come, Woudiver." He led the way to the black car, through the hastily retreating onlookers.

Woudiver hulked himself within and lay groaning in a heap. Anacho started the vehicle and they departed the oval plaza.

Chapter 21

They drove to the shed. The technicians, in the absence of Deine Zarre, had not reported for work. The shed felt dead and abandoned; the space-boat, which had seemed on the verge of coming alive, lay desolate on its chocks.

The three marshaled Woudiver within, as they might lead a cantankerous bull, and tied him between two posts, Woudiver making a continual moaning complaint.

Reith watched him a moment. Woudiver was not yet expendable. Certainly he was still dangerous. For all his display and expostulation, he watched Reith with a clever and hard gaze.

"Woudiver," said Reith, "you have worked great harm upon me."

Woudiver's great body became racked with sobbing; he seemed a monstrous and ugly baby. "You plan to torment me, and kill me."

"The thought has presented itself," Reith admitted. "But I have more urgent desires. To finish the ship and return to Earth with news of this hellish planet I would even forgo the pleasure of your death."

"In that case," said Woudiver, suddenly businesslike, "all is as before. Pay over the money, and we will proceed."

Reith's jaw hung in disbelief. He laughed in admiration for Woudiver's wonderful insouciance.

Anacho and Traz were less amused. Anacho poked the great belly with a stick. "What of last night?" he demanded in a suave voice. "Do you recall your conduct? What of the electric probes, and the wicker harness?"

"What of Deine Zarre, the two children?" spoke Traz.

Woudiver looked appealingly toward Reith. "Whose words carry weight?"

Reith chose his words carefully. "All of us have cause for resentment. You would be a fool to expect ease and conviviality."

"Indeed, he shall suffer," said Traz through gritted teeth.

"You shall live," said Reith, "but only to serve our interests. I don't care a bice for your life unless you make yourself useful."

Again in Woudiver's eyes Reith discerned a cold and crafty glint. "So it shall be," said Woudiver.

"I want you to hire a competent replacement for Deine Zarre, at once."

"Expensive, expensive," said Woudiver. "We were lucky in Zarre."

"The responsibility for his absence is yours," said Reith.

"No one goes through life without making mistakes," Woudiver admitted. "This was one of mine. But I know just the man. He will come high, I warn you."

"Money is no object," said Reith. "We want the best. Secondly, I want you to summon the technicians back to work. All by telephone, of course."

"No difficulties whatever," declared Woudiver heartily. "The work will proceed with dispatch."

"You must arrange immediate delivery of the materials and supplies yet needed. And you must pay all costs and salaries incurred henceforth."

"What?" roared Woudiver.

"Further," said Reith, "you will remain tied between these posts. For your sustenance you must pay a thousand—or better, two thousand—sequins each day."

"*What!*" cried Woudiver. "Do you think to cheat and bewilder poor Woudiver?"

"Do you agree to the conditions?" Reith asked. "If not I will ask Anacho and Traz to kill you, and both of them bear you grudges."

Woudiver drew himself to his full height. "I agree," he said in a stately voice. "And now, since it seems that I must sponsor your hallucinations and suffer backbreaking expense in the bargain, let us instantly get to work. The moment I see you vanish into space will be a happy one, I assure you! Now then, release these chains so that I may go to the telephone."

"Stay where you are," said Reith. "We will bring the telephone to you. And now, where is your money?"

"You can't be serious," Woudiver exclaimed.

THE END